Adventures of Death, Reincarnation and Annihilation

Francis H. Powell

For information, or to order additional copies, please contact:

Beacon Publishing Group
P.O. Box 41573 Charleston, S.C. 29423
800.817.8480| beaconpublishinggroup.com

Publisher's catalog available by request.

ISBN-13: 978-1-949472-01-1

ISBN-10: 978-1-949472-01

Published in 2019. New York, NY 10001.

First Edition. Printed in the USA.

THE MASTER'S HOUSE

Part one

The strange goings on in the life of Amos Toft.

We had found her face down on the sand, as the tide closed in. The moon shed silvery light and there was a soft gentle offshore breeze that glanced our faces. We'd run out of our house, having seen torch light. They had left as quickly as they had arrived. There were sounds of horses, leaving at speed, shadowy figures, hooded, dressed like soldiers, soon fading into the horizon. We presumed she was dead and were relieved when she spluttered and coughed and fought for breath.

"Let's get her inside" my wife said urgently. She was totally naked and had no possessions.

"Are you all right?" I demanded. She did not respond. I repeated myself again, there was just the sound of her heavy labored breathing.

"She appears in terrible shock" my wife said, as we helped her up. We draped one of her arms over my wife's shoulders while I propped the other. We struggled along the sand and then headed towards our small house, which looked over the large bay.

"What's your name?" I asked, expecting by now she was in some kind of condition to speak. Again no response, her eyes were fixed on the ground, she made no attempt to speak. We got her back to the house and sat her down on a couch.

What had happened? Why had she been left naked on the sand, as the tide came in? What was going through her mind? My wife got a towel and offered it to her to clean her and cover her naked body.

"She will have to stay the night, it is late, at least she will be safe here," my wife said before searching for some clothes. I hardly dared not look at her. She was evidently young, very beautiful, with long flaxen hair that cascaded down her back.

"Water" I asked, "do you want some water?" Again there was no response, she did not even look at the glass of water, her eyes never veering away from the ground, as if she was locked in a trance. My wife returned holding a white night dress. It was far from a perfect fit, the woman was far taller and a different shape from my wife.

"Put it on" said my wife, holding out the night dress. The woman took it slowly and slipped it on. I explained to my wife that I had tried to offer water; my wife suggested perhaps she was hungry. My wife said softly "Food, do you want food?" There was again no reply to this latest offer.

"Perhaps she has had an accident" said my wife with a sigh, "perhaps she just wants to sleep, she has been traveling possibly on a tiring journey."

"What naked!" I said dubiously.

"Yes that is a bit unusual" agreed my wife, adding, "and those men on horses holding torches, who were they?"

"I have no idea," I replied, "but to leave a naked woman on an empty beach, is not normal!"

My wife turned to the young woman, with a face of desperation in search of some kind of response.

"Can you explain, who you are, what you are doing here, who those men were?"

I added, some words of comfort "you are safe here with us, we won't hurt you."

The young girl was doubled up on the couch, her arms tightly holding her legs, posing as if she was protecting herself.

Her head did not even turn in either the direction of my wife or me. Was she deaf or mute? Or perhaps she came from foreign lands.

My wife realizing our efforts to aid the girl were fruitless said,

"I suggest we leave her and let her sleep, perhaps in the morning she will be ready to speak."

My wife got some blankets and we left the young woman still in the same position, presuming at some point she would settle down and get some sleep. I bolted the front door and blew out the candles, leaving the room shrouded in darkness. Both my wife and I called out a cordial "goodnight" as we went upstairs to settle down for the night.

We felt assured that the young woman would not take flight in the middle of the night. After all we lived in such a remote place. This was our choice. We did not want too much contact with other people. We were self-contained, in our rather insular world. We had a field at the back of the house, where we kept a few farm animals, goats, pigs, and chickens, we grew a lot of vegetables, other than this the sea provided for most of our needs. We rarely strayed from our home, sometimes we would take our cart and buy things at the market of the nearest town. We had lived in this remote house for about ten years.

It had belonged to my parents. They were relatively rich and used this house as a kind of summer retreat. I recall spending a number of idyllic summers there, until tragedy struck when my father never came back from a fishing trip, having been swept away into a raging sea. My mother never recovered from this and her love for this house, turned to bitterness.

It was also no place to bring up a young family, it was so isolated and loneliness was sure to set in, augmenting her intense grief.

The house was left vacant for many years. She took her young family, me and younger brother Rolf to the live exclusively in the city. She remarried but died giving birth. I was brought up along with Rolf, by my aunt Magda, since the pain of my mother's death being too much for Randolf, our stepfather, who couldn't stand the thought of us being around, it only served to deepen his grief.

Magda was older than my mother. A corpulent woman, who lived for cooking, eating and telling wondrous stories about her adventurous past. She was married to a man who was quite her opposite, a man deep and intense, whose volatile moods changed in an instant. Sometimes he could be as sweet as father had been, other times an insatiable anger surfaced from nowhere.

It was clear to Rolf and I that Uncle Kurt, resented us being thrust upon his household. He had no interest in children, he was only interested in his own affairs. He would take his leather belt to us, if ever we did something to displease him. Magda would make pleas on our behalf, but they were always brushed aside.

Both Aunt Magda and Uncle Kurt had acquired dubious reputations around the city. Magda was seen as an enchantress, people were wary of her. When she was younger she had been a dancer, or so she led us to believe. When she fell during an epic performance, she was forced to give up dancing. She would often rejoice in the fact that she had travelled the globe performing in front of large audiences. She would often talk beaming with pride of travelling to far off lands, dancing in front of Kings and noblemen, each performance earning rapturous applause. Whenever she concluded telling stories of adventures, she would always end by breaking out into fits of laughter, causing us to doubt that there was in truth in her improbable anecdotes. We never saw her dance or indeed any evidence that she was the dancer she claimed to be.

She insisted when she could no longer perform she began to cook and eat hefty meals and began to put on weight. Her body no longer served her as a dancer, so food became her refuge.

When she met Uncle Kurt, she was still slim and nimble, as well as having the temerity to engage with this man who had an intimidating aura.

Kurt was once a humble worker, cleaning the hospital floors. He then worked as a hospital porter, escorting in and outpatients, from their operations. One night, when working as a porter he spent the entire night conversing with an elderly man, who was at the point of death. The elderly man was wise and seemed urgently trying to convey his knowledge during his final hours to Kurt, who happily listened to all he had to say. The man talked of places that Kurt should go to, in order to acquire, as he put it "special powers".

He gave Kurt a book, one of the old man's few possessions, full of scribbled notes of the man's own hand. He told Kurt to read it carefully because the book contained the keys to enlightenment. Why he had entrusted so much in a lowly hospital worker, was open to conjecture. As light broke the two men were still in deep conversation, until the old man slipped into unconsciousness.

This encounter seemed to change Kurt's life. It was like he adopted a new persona. He left his job and left the city to go on an extensive journey, in which he gathered many things enlisted in the old man's book. He lived off the land and travelled far and wide, living like a hermit.

At a point he chose to re-enter civilization and return to the city he had spent most of his life. People were surprised by the marked change in him. Rumors spread that he had somehow acquired healing powers.

Long suffering widower Liv Lunt went to visit Kurt, as her chronic skin condition showed no sign of abating. Kurt administered a mixture of honey, bees wax, and olive oil on the woman's irritated skin. Within days the widower's face seemed to glow with a natural freshness.

Word began to spread of Kurt's newly acquired gift, and one day Jan Henriksen, the richest man in the city, having got wind of Liv Lund's remarkable transformation, arrived in search of a cure for the warts that covered his face. Kurt's room was full of jars and he reached into one and grabbed a handful of blister beetles, with a mortar and pestle he managed to make a compound of cantharidin. He said he would pay Kurt well, if he was suitably cured.

Once again Kurt proved to be the solution to the man's ailment. Clients of a higher standing similar to Henriksen, followed. Not all were cured, some were left bitter as there was no obvious improvement to their ailment. It was Kurt's rising reputation however that caused the first encounter between him and Aunt Magda. According to Magda, who as I mentioned earlier was far reliable, as she often mixed truth randomly with fiction, it was just after her terrible fall. Hobbling into Kurt's humble abode stacked full of miscellaneous quirky objects, she stopped to draw in the sight of Kurt, who for the first ten minutes of their meeting hardly afforded her a glance, despite the fact that she was wearing her prettiest summer frock. At first Magda took this badly, but after a time she realized that in Kurt, she had found a challenge, if she was to break his cold exterior and

pronounced indifference towards her. She was
(according to her) at this time, more accustomed
to fending off men's advances and on quite a
number of occasions the odd offer of marriage
and yet here was a man who disinterested by her.
He said nothing as she took a seat
resting her crutches against the wall.
'Don't you speak to your patients' she demanded,
breaking the silence.
'When necessary' he replied, his head bent down,
eyes fixed on his desk, as if he was perusing a
complicated problem.
'Did you hear of my fall, perhaps, it was in all
the papers'. She demanded, a slight smile on her
face, as she delighted in her notoriety.
Kurt shrugged his shoulders and frowned.
'I am not concerned with such things, what is
your name Madame' he replied still untouched by
Magda's feminine charms.
'I am Magda Rask, you must of heard of me, my
reputation as a dancer is known worldwide,' she
crowed while running her hand through her long
blond hair.
He gave her a blank look, his insouciance
obvious.
'I don't believe I have, now how can I help you, I
am a busy man.'
Magda showed him the disfigured ankle brought
about when she had un-ceremonially fell, after
miscuing a firebird leap, ending off the stage, to
the absolute shock of the audience.

He gave her ankle an almost derogatory glance.
'What do you expect me to do, you have seen
physicians about this injury I suppose.'
She had expected him to perform a miraculous
cure, to have her quickly back on stage, but he
seemed to be totally dispassionate about her
situation.
'I have heard that you have special healing
powers, why you even managed to rid Jan
Henriksen of his warts.'
Kurt frowned.
'I might have cured his unsightly skin disease,
that much is true, but your ankle, needs a
different type of healing, only a trained surgeon
can provide.'
She looked at him, her disappointment obvious.
Despite his refusal to attend to her damaged
ankle, she tried to remain resolute in order to
strike up some rapport.
The conversation that followed between the two
remained stagnated, that was until Magda boldly
said, 'well if you won't see to my damaged
ankle, you can at least marry me, by way of
compensation.'
Kurt didn't appreciate her flippancy, he glared at
her testily. He snarled,
'I find your jest tasteless Madame, I am a busy
man, I suggest you leave.'
Slowly she got up, but as she did she feigned
falling over and being in great pain. He was
forced to come to her aid, to assist her standing

up. As he did so, the two ended up in a tight embrace. For the first time in his life Kurt felt a sudden wave of passion for a woman, his stiff manner melted away. Was it her strong perfume that brought about this change? She'd been given it by a French count, who was desperate to win her favor.

Whatever proceeded Aunt Magda would not elaborate, she would, as was her way burst into hysterical laughter, again causing us to doubt the authenticity of her story. However it is true to say that Magda and Kurt did marry within weeks of meeting one another.

Not all Kurt's endeavors were met with approval, particularly some his female clientele. Birgit Schwantz known as one of the most beautiful women in the locality had found her shingles worsening, to such an extent she was forced to cancel all her oncoming social events. Kurt had applied a fine paste of leaves of Indian lilac over the affected area, it had worked well for him before, but for some inexplicable reason this time his efforts proved abject.

It became apparent that Magda, overcome with jealousy did not appreciate beautiful women crossing their fresh hold and was administering some kind of counter magic. Both Kurt and Magda found their reputations tarnished. People still came for Kurt's assistance, but now it was more out of desperation, when they found absolutely no alternative. Women shied away from Magda, for fear she might unleash some dark magic that would diminish their beauty

Both Rolf and I were fearful of Kurt. He seemed to be able control people, play with their minds. He seemed a complex mixture of personalities.
We would often go to sleep to sound of him shouting at Aunt Magda. We even suspected he struck her on occasion, though she would never admit as much.

At the earliest possibility, having secured a job, and having convinced Magda I could look after Rolf, until he finished his schooling, we left the household. Magda was sad at losing us, but seemed to understand our motives, Kurt was getting even more difficult, his mind verging on insanity.

Rolf and I would occasionally visit our uncle and aunt's house. Both were still the same, although uncle Kurt was perhaps further detached from reality, muttering under his breath, cursing Rolf and I, still wearing his night clothes, while he a read a rugged looking threadbare book with strong intent.

One day when Rolf and I forced ourselves to pay them a visit, we were surprised to find the house looking in an obviously dormant state. It looked like it was derelict. Aunt Magda's garden was overgrown and had obviously been unattended to, in many months.

We went up to the front door and knocked. Normally Aunt Magda would shuffle over to the door and open it with delight as she appreciated our visits, but our constant banging on the door proved to be of no avail.

We decided to see if the neighbors could spread some light on the situation. Bente Grun, knew of all significant happenings in the neighborhood and spent her time surveying all that was going on from her bay window. We didn't want to approach this elderly shrew concerning the absence of our uncle and aunt, but given that there wc were limited in choice, nobody else had responded to us, we hesitantly knocked at her door.

Having opened her door she stared at us for a moment before demanding why we had broken her afternoon rest. We explained that we were concerned for our uncle and aunt. "Haven't seen for ages, not for ages" she repeated endlessly in this voice that was barely decipherable, as her mouth was filled with ulcers, much larger than peas. While we walked away she still kept on repeating "not for ages" until her voice diminished out of earshot. She'd always hated Aunt Magda and Kurt even more so. She saw the pair of them as being "ungodly" while maliciously spreading rumors that they were in league with the devil himself. If Kurt in his wisdom had cured her ulcers, her perception of them might have been otherwise. He prescribed

Swiss sage, but her pain persisted and her speech became more and more impaired, but not to the extent she couldn't bad-mouth Kurt and my aunt. We couldn't fully rely on her word, so we decided we would return another day to see if we try to locate them.

As we made our way to the house again we met by chance Abner Kuntz, who knew our aunt well, indeed was one of her few friends. Abner had always cherished Aunt Magda, to the extent we imagined he was secretly in love with her. Kurt resented his presence in his house and made it clear to all. Abner would make Magda laugh, something Kurt never did. Even Rolf and I liked him, he was so different to Kurt, telling us stories that were as outlandish as Aunt Magda's yarns. Abner had spent a lot of his life at sea, he lived for travel and adventure, or so he said.

He claimed he met Magda, when she did a dance in front of the Prince of Moldavia, while he tutored the young prince's sons in the art of sailing. Of course both Abner and Magda had laughed and laughed, with tears in their eyes, at the conclusion of this tale. More to the truth Abner had spent a lonesome life as a fisherman, like Aunt Magda he was a total masquerader, who liked to play on our naivety.

As he walked back from work, smelling of fish, while smoking a clay pipe, we accosted him.

His eyes sparkled as he caught sight of us.

"Hello you two, haven't seen you around these parts in a long time."

"We were concerned for our uncle and aunt" I replied more solemnly, as Abner's look transformed into a much graver one.

"Haven' t you heard, nobody has seen them for a long time, I even got the police to enter their house, the house was totally deserted." He said drawing a big intake of smoke.

"Did Aunt Magda talk about leaving with Uncle Kurt?" I demanded.

"Not a word, your Uncle Kurt has been going increasingly insane, there was less and less demand for his healing methods, but your aunt seemed to be coping."

We went to a café and spent some time with Abner, who was the last link we had to our aunt. We discussed old times spent with Aunt Magda. Before leaving us Abner said "she loved you boys, she did and she loved telling you those stories of hers." He laughed profusely as he got up and hobbled home to his stark home that looked out on the sea. No doubt he had dreams of Magda dancing before some royalty or other.

A few months later we heard from Abner that the house where we had spent much of childhood had been inexplicably burnt to the ground. The police had no idea how this had come to pass, nobody including the local snoop Bente Grun had seen any suspicious activity. Arson was of course much discussed, Kurt had his antagonists, but there was no evidence to support this. The land was bought by a rich land agent and within no time the last traces of Kurt and Magda were now obliterated, as a new house sprung up and young family moved in.

When I met Inga, my wife I was working for a law firm, while she was studying. I told her one evening as we walked arm in arm along the riverfront, bathed in glowing moonlight, that my family had a house, by the coast. She was immediately intrigued and had romantic notions of what the house might look like, so we decided to travel there, as soon as the weather was suitably clement. I told her it would be a dilapidated state, but her enthusiasm to discover this mysterious house by the sea outweighed thoughts the derelict condition the house would be in.

When we finally arrived after a long journey, drawing in the pungent smells of seaweed and the distant sounds of waves crashing towards the shore, *we* fell in love with the place immediately. It felt strange as I unlocked the door and we hesitantly entered. The windows had been boarded up and when light flooded in, the full extent of the houses dilapidated condition was revealed. The house was coated by a thick layer of dust, the air was stagnant, punctuated by the distinctive smell of mold and decay. Everywhere was markedly grimy mildewed. There were intricate networks of cobwebs which had adjoined themselves around the chairs and other furniture, which had been ravaged by termites, beetles and fungi. Everything looked as if it had been locked in a time warp.

It took us time to clean up and revitalize this dank ramshackle shell of a house. I had patchy memories of the place, its timbers black with pitch, the large verandah at the front, my parent's room with windows that looked out to sea and a bed my father had made from driftwood. The poky room I shared for a while with my younger brother. There were the pagan figurines in the back garden, that was strewn with shingle, with plants and herbs poking through, the flower beds being aligned with flint and scallop-shells.

.   It was summertime and we decided to swim in the sea. We were of course totally alone, it was like having our own kingdom, our own utopia, away from disease and pestilence, away from the guts and other refuse all thrown on the street causing an unbearable odor, the residences and factories, tenements and shops, all regularly belching thick clouds of black soot into the city's air. The dark, circuitous alleys coupled with tall, shadowy buildings, that were havens to pick pockets and other criminal types, who would slit your throat for a scrap of bread. All of this would be exchanged for boundless freedom. It just seemed to make sense. Inga would take her books, I would have to adapt to new life, learn how to live off the land and sea.

We would have to work on the house to make it habitable, I would have to learn the skills of an artisan, to be able to achieve the necessary repairs to make it more habitable. There was nothing standing in our way. My resignation and explanation for my departure from the law firm, was met with consternation. I was giving up my career in exchange for a pastoral life, of which nobody could see the benefits.

My brother Rolf at this point in time was living in the colonies and had no interest in the house. He didn't have any association with it, as he was an infant, when father died. Rolf had made money and was happy for us to move to the remote house by the sea. Having received his blessing, we began planning our future, moving our possessions.

It was hard at first, learning to fish and forage, for sloe-backed mussels clusters of shellfish, shrimp, cockles, sea beet and rock samphire, curling sea beet and fat ribbons of seaweed the beach and nearby estuary becoming our larder. It certainly made a difference, from working behind an office desk.

Each day was a bit of a discovery. We had happily traded the squalor of the city for a life of being able to sustain ourselves but were always susceptible to the whims of nature. Of course we could not live off the sea alone. Inga taught herself to bake bread, and we turned our attention to the overgrown grassy area. I had vague memories of father growing vegetables, but when we arrived the garden inevitably was a mass of weeds and a dense network of brambles. Once I had cleared the area, we went to the nearest market town and bought seeds. Time passed and we brought some chickens. Our scope for producing food began to evolve, we were soon practically self-contained, we hardly lacked for anything, other people's company was an unnecessary requirement, Inga had her books and me my tasks to keep me busy.

Part Two
A Strange Awakening

I woke up in the middle of the night, really parched. I slowly ambled out of the bedroom, still almost in a dreamlike state. As I looked down from the top of the landing, I was forced to check my momentum. There she was, not fast asleep as I anticipated, but fully awake, doing slow dance movements, as light was beginning to break, illuminating the bay. She was at the same time singing a song gently under her breath, whispering it, with great deliberation, for her own delectation. My body totally tensed up, I knew a mere creek of the floor would draw her attention to me and this moment would be lost forever. I angled my body in such a way as to not be seen.

She made deft gestures with a repertoire of intricate, flowing patterns, her arms doing loops, her head and torso faster bending and twisting movements. I was captivated, while rooted to the spot. She was totally naked and occasionally her fingers would niftily glance over her nipples, which were erect, her long flowing hair swept through the air, sometimes obscuring her face. I felt I was an intruder, in my own house; she was in her element, very much alive, prevailing in her surroundings. It wasn't a dance for any kind of audience, perhaps she was adorning nature, or perhaps she was reliving a happy moment of her past, a dance to impress a former lover? It was such a rich beautiful priceless intimate moment. I could see seagulls venture closer to the house, their calls sometimes obliterating her softly sung gentle melodies, but she carried on as if she was possessed.

My hypnotic state was broken as I heard my wife cough; perhaps she had awoken and was conscious of absence. I crept back in the bedroom, leaving the young woman, I imagined dancing. My wife was awake, however still sleep laden. I muttered that I had woken with a strong thirst. I still had this strong thirst my mind occupied, reminiscing, reliving that dance I had encroached upon. Somehow I managed to capture some sleep.

My wife and I went downstairs to prepare some breakfast. The young woman was in a crumpled heap, a blanket covering her, in a deep enduring sleep. Even the occasional clatter of cutlery on plates, muffled conversations, could not disturb her.

There was a pressing issue, we had to take action, the young woman could not remain with us indefinitely, she was after all an intruding on our secluded existence. Maybe once awake she might naturally take flight, without any prompting, if not we would have to urge her to come with us to the nearest town, where upon she could be left in the hands of the authorities. It was a strange situation all round. My wife was of a pragmatic mind, I was still captivated by what I had seen in the early hours, that dance. As we discussed this matter more intently, the young woman showed no sign of stirring from her comatose state, sometimes she would let out strained sighs, her mind vexed, as if she was having a nightmare. My wife and I went about some mundane tasks, as habitually we did, such as cleaning, digging up vegetables, making some necessary repairs, waiting for her to rouse.

While I was outside, seeing to a door that had loosened from its hinges, I heard my wife talking, obviously conversing with the young woman, who had finally awoken. It seemed like she was coaxing her to eat some food.

My wife looked troubled. She said desperately "She won't eat and she still does not want to talk." She shook her head ruefully. The young girl seemed to be staring out to sea, as if the conversation had nothing to do with her. So nothing had changed since the night before, we were still confronted with somebody who would never respond to our questions. We were still facing the same dilemma, of what do. My wife soon lost her patience.

She turned face on to the young girl and said in her most forthright voice, "right, we are taking you to the nearest town and the authorities will deal with you, we can't harbor you here, it's simply not right." She shook her head, there was an unusual determination visible in her eyes.

Tears began to well up in the young girl's eyes. She began gasping for breath, like she had suddenly been struck by some fatal respiratory condition. Soon she was in a state trauma, wailing in agony, howling in distress, the volume of noise augmenting dramatically. My wife and I were at a loss, what should we do? I had never witnessed somebody in such a state, her whole body in this frenzied tortured state. I had been to funerals that were far less intense than this. I imagined that to take this young girl we would have to force her to leave, she was now entrenched in our house and we felt powerless to eject her. Even my wife's determination seemed to be fading and she seemed to be softening to the young girls cause. Though no words passed out of the young girl's mouth, she sent us looks that seemed to be pleading for her to stay, as if her very life depended on it.

Suddenly I was able to make out a voice, the voice of a young girl,
"Please this is my rightful place."
I turned in the direction of my wife.

"Did you hear her" I said abruptly, she said something."
My wife looked at me nonplussed, saying incredulously, "what are you talking about, she is just hysterical, but she has not so much as uttered a word, you are imagining things Amos." Despite my wife's disbelief, I was sure the young woman had communicated with me. The proof came a few moments later, as more words entered my head,
"convince her, I beg of you, I can't be torn from here, nor from you."

It was the same young woman's voice, it was desperate and urgent, resonating in my head. The voice seemed to be exclusively in my head and my wife seemed unable to pick up on the young girl's desperate voice. I had never heard voices in my head; I was shaken by this new development.

My wife turned to me and shrugged, "I suppose she can stay for a while." The tension that had braced the young girl, disappeared and she hugged my wife. My wife fought to be free from her embrace. "That's enough of that" said my wife testily shunning the young girl's affection and gratitude. The young girl seemed to retain this vow of silence, bar the words that had ghosted into my head. She still refused to eat and seemed content just to stare out sea, while lain on the veranda, deep in her own seclusion.

My wife and I got on with our usual tasks of sustaining the house, my wife uncomfortable with this new situation. As the sun lowered beyond the horizon, my wife and I prepared a dinner, for three people, expecting the young girl's resistance to eating to be broken. As we beckoned her into the dining area, with three places set, she just shook her head and continued to stare out to sea, as the light closed in. My wife placed some next to her, with the hope she would eat it later.

Hardly a word was said between myself and my wife as we picked at our dinner, in a subdued atmosphere. After we had cleared away the dinner, she came in the house, positioning herself by a window and again she appeared to assume her disposition of being enchanted by the sea, as moonlight flooded the crashing waves that frothed and spumed with a hypnotic frequency.

My wife prepared some blankets and nightclothes and when we were ready to retire to bed, we said goodnight, but of course she offered no spoken response, just a slight shift of her head, as some kind of recognition.

I found it hard to sleep, while my wife drifted easily into a deep sleep. Suddenly amongst the sound of my wife's rhythmic heavy breathing I heard the sound of gentle footsteps walking up the stairs, then in the direction of our bedroom, stopping short of the door to our bedroom which was slightly ajar. Obscured by the door, but I knew she was there, but why? Was I being beckoned to witness one of her enthralling dances? What did she want of me? Whatever, I was rooted to the bed, constrained by the fact that I might disturb my wife's deep sleep and could ill afford to be seen colluding with the young girl.

It didn't take much time before her voice once again penetrated my head.
"I'm with child" she said softly in voice laced with joy and fervor, adding "of course it's your child."

I managed to strangle any words that would surely have woken my wife, who in turn would have thought I was mad, talking to the darkness. Many thoughts streamed through my mind. Was she making some kind of cruel jest, she must have noticed my wife was now almost beyond childbearing years and that we were obviously a childless couple. In fact after years of trying, our hopes had withered away and with it our love. This had turned our relationship into one of companionship, our union still strong, because of our love for our house.

We'd tried everything; we made love during the lunar phase my wife was born into, which we perceived as her most fertile time. She wore a wooden pendant with a bind rune to rouse her fertility. We'd even gone down some outlandish routes, trying to appease the spirits of fertility, having drenched my wife with the blood of a bull, we made love, but again it was the same fruitless result.

I'd dreamed of a child growing up in this special house, the rich surroundings adorned by the sea. My wife would have made such a natural mother, the cruelty of her empty womb, was a dark endless journey hard to bare. And now this. Of course it was absurd, there had been no physical contact between us. I tried to reassure myself, I was hearing a voice in my head that was all, my mind playing cruel tricks. "Did you hear me, I'm to have your child" the voice reiterated, this time with an edge of desperation. What could I do? If she could communicate with me in such a way, then perhaps I could do the same with her, place my thoughts in her head. "Who are you and why are you doing this?" my mind diffused. However she did not respond, she could get inside my head, but I was unable to do the same. I slowly levered myself out of bed, trying to avoid awakening my wife. I walked as lightly as I could to the door and slipped out of the room. There she was naked, as I'd anticipated just behind the door. I gestured for her to go downstairs. When out of earshot form my sleeping wife I said in an urgent voice, "for the love of God, put some clothes on."

More of her words entered my head "Your seed is in my belly, dear husband, don't you want to touch my belly?"

"For God's sake my wife sleeps upstairs," I protested adding and besides, "we have never bedded."

The young girl looked wounded and imparted "don't make light of our love, nor our unborn child"

"Who are you?" I asked angrily.

"You know who I am dear husband, I know I was taken from you a long time ago, my name is Astrid."

Her name meant nothing to me. I wondered if she was a woman who'd been dispatched from an asylum, left on the beach, now wielding her insane notions on our household.

"What do you want from me?" I asked with a troubled voice.

"To live together in this our house, to carry on our love and to bring up this child, that will complete our joy."

"This is insane!" I said, "I don't know you and I have a wife, as well you know."

I was trying to reason with a woman, who refused to speak, but who seemed able to send messages to my mind.

"She is not your real wife," the young girl transmitted, "she has been sent to confuse you, take you away from me, I am your rightful wife, she must leave or be killed by you."

"This has got to stop" I said in a hushed but firm voice, fearful that my wife would be aroused and find me talking in the middle of the night with this young girl. "It is better that you leave, our house now, find yourself a new place to dwell, you are no longer welcome here."
"I can't leave either this house, nor you my dear husband, your heart might be cold, but as our child grows in my belly, it will thaw and our long lost love will burn strong, once again."
Suddenly she grabbed my hand and placed it on her belly. I didn't retract my hand, as I would have imagined I would. If indeed there was a baby, it would be of the minutest proportions, as she hadn't appeared to show any signs. But for some unfathomable reason I felt compelled to keep my hand placed on her belly. More than this I was starting to feel something towards the unborn child and its mother no less, despite the fact that I was totally disconnected from its conception.
I finally withdrew my hand, tears streamed from her eyes.
"Perhaps I spoke too hastily" I said contritely, "you can stay, under our roof, but for charitable reasons, and you must not hurt my wife in any way." Of course my wife would never get to hear the young girl's wild proclamations, but they would be lodged in my mind. I went back to bed with my wife, again exercising the utmost discretion not to wake her up. Fortunately as I

lay my head on my pillow, I found her still deep
in sleep, almost as if she'd been stupefied.

       The days that ensued followed a
similar pattern. My wife and I going about our
usual business, the young girl, or Astrid as she
had conveyed to me, would spend her days,
gazing out to sea, as she seemed prone to do,
there was no form of communication between us,
but an underlying tension seemed to simmer in
the house, my wife eyeing her with suspicion, no
doubt willing her departure.

       One morning we came downstairs to
find her with her body arched over vomiting. My
wife quickly concluded this was due to lack of
nutrition, but I knew different of course.
"She's pregnant" I said to my wife, who looked
at me in stark amazement.
"How do you know?" demanded my wife, with a
look of surprise.
"She's obviously suffering from morning
sickness," I said trying to convey an air of
intuition rather than knowledge of her situation.
I thought this would be the cue for my wife to
begin the hastened process of dispatching the girl
to a new home, a nunnery for young girls who
find themselves in such a condition, after all I
could not imagine her wanting a pregnant woman
under her roof, it would prove a daily cruel
reminder of our deficiency in producing a child.
No words of such nature seemed forthcoming;
indeed she seemed to be offering herself to the

young girl as a source of comfort. Perhaps there was a feeling of sisterhood between the two, something I hadn't anticipated. It seemed like my wife was prepared to nurse the young girl through her pregnancy, while Astrid, as only I knew her, wished her dead. I was left in the middle of this enigma. My wife had enlightened herself in the event of getting pregnant, which of course had never happened, but it had seemed a necessary precaution at the time, living in such a remote area. The tense atmosphere that had gripped the house since the young girl's arrival relented.

The young girl even chose to eat with us. My wife gave her herrings, sardines, kelp, lentils, black beans, chickpeas, sweet potatoes, any food that she thought would help with the unborn baby's growth. She made tea using nettle or red raspberry leaf, which she said would strengthen the womb. She built an altar, placing a purple satin cloth over it, with some ceremonial rose scented candles placed at the four corners. She placed some stones including moonstone, malachite, rose quartz. She also put some silver keys, which she said would unlock the birth passage, allowing for an easy birth. She would burn cinnamon incense claiming it was an herb of good fortune, health and protection.

One day I caught her drawing the signs of a goddess and a god on Astrid's belly, a goddess on her left, the god on her right with

honeysuckle oil. She insisted the young girl take plenty of rest, enforcing her own paradigm. She was taking so much trouble, and I couldn't help but wonder why.
I was also still mystified by the young, Astrid. I hungered to know of her origins.

I found it hard to sleep most nights. Would Astrid try to communicate with me, was she dancing, was she holding a vigil just behind the door of my wife my bedroom? Would she claim me as hers again?

One night I managed to drift off into a deep sleep and with this sleep came a strong vivid dream. It was nighttime and a there was a storm, the wind swept across the shoreline. No ships could sail on such a night. I saw my house being battered by the force of the gale. But surprised me more was the fact that my house was surrounded by other houses, indeed it was in the midst of what looked like a thriving fishing village. Over the brow of the hill-topped peninsula, came men on horseback. Their arrival was sudden and before any alarm could be raised they set about destroying all the houses with their inhabitants. Flaming arrows shot by archers on horseback. Those men who managed to flee their houses in time, were struck down by swords, the women were dragged away, no doubt to be raped or horribly abused.

The village was carnage, every
house set on fire. Through the din of destruction,
a shout broke through.
"We have come to take the young woman, give
her to us and we will leave you unharmed."
Suddenly I appeared standing on the verandah of
my house, in front of the band of men on
horseback. I was in abject fear. I knew it was
me, but it seemed like an earlier incarnation, I
seemed to be in a different time period. The
leader of the band of men repeated his demand. I
could see myself helplessly pleading with the
man, but to no avail. I saw myself re-enter the
house and come out with Astrid. She was
gripping to me tightly beseeching me not to hand
her over to the men, but I knew I was helpless
and was obliged to give in to their demands. The
leader of the band of men dismounted and tore
her away from me. She was tied on the back of a
horse and taken away at speed, she shouted to
me, "Wait for me, I'll be back, you have to wait
for me, my love," her voice quickly trailed away
as the men were soon over the brow of the hill, as
the village burnt to the ground, without trace.

I sat on the verandah, my mind in
torment, engulfed in smoke, until I reached the
point where everything went totally hazy. My
dream was moving on, there was the advent of a
new one. The haziness cleared. I found myself in
bed. It was nighttime. Suddenly I heard gentle
footsteps approaching. It was like I was

reenacting what had happened before with
Astrid, perhaps my mind was re-assimilating
what had occurred. The door was slowly opened.
However this time it was not Astrid who
appeared, it was my wife. She was totally naked,
but she had some beads around her neck, silver
beads representing the lunar months, purple ones
are for the eight sabbaths, four beads for the
cardinal elements, three different beads
symbolizing the realms of earth, sea and sky.

On her head she wore a headdress, a
pentagram resting on her temple, silver edged
amethyst beads and little crystals, all attached on
a silver chain. She didn't speak to me and I
seemed paralyzed and unable to speak with her.

Her face and body were as youthful
as the day I had taken a young shy girl to bed, for
the first time on our wedding night. Her breasts
were not saggy as I had got used to in recent
years but were firm and shapely. The lines on
face that had appeared in recent years, with onset
of middle age set in, were not visible, her skin
flushed with the freshness of youth.
Equally surprising was what happened next. She
stood straight with a slight bend of the knees,
slowly raising her arms up to the ceiling with the
palms of her hands facing each other, I soon
realized she was about to begin a dance. The only
time I'd seen her dance before was on our
wedding night. Two fiddlers had started a
wedding reel and as was expected of us we'd

danced to the first tune, rather gingerly, it was the first and last time we'd danced together.

Her dance followed a circle, she went six times anti clockwise, her dance involving snaky abdominal and hip movements, drops, and beautiful turns, as well as hand gestures, and head and eye movements. Once she had completed her six anti clockwise circles, she reversed and went clockwise, keeping the same pattern. I imagined if Astrid was looking on, she would have been devastated at having to admire my wife's sassy, strong, and decidedly feminine movements. It was clearly evident the two women were now in conflict and the trophy they were fighting over was me. As the dance continued hypnotically, it almost seemed like my wife was floating, she her body weightless and almost evanescent. Words suddenly entered into my consciousness, "Amos you are mine, I would never let you go" the words repeated in my head, going around and round as if in tandem with the dance. I did not see her voice the words, she seemed to be able to transmit them somehow, in the same way Astrid could, more than this the sound of her voice almost replicated the sweet voice of Astrid. When the realization of what she was dancing around hit me, I screamed. It was the head of Astrid, placed on a silver platter, surrounded by amaranth flowers, shells and stones. I bolted forward, now fully awake. My wife was leaning over me, in her hand there was a damp towel.

"You suddenly came down with a fever in the middle of the night" she said adding "you've been delirious for the last hour or so." I was certainly perspiring and felt incredibly weak, but this did not stop me noticing a big change in my wife. Gone were the dowdy smock, she typically wore, replaced by a dress she had not worn since about the time I first met her. It was a flowery dress, which I remember at the time I told her it really suited her. The dress was one thing, her face looked like it had lost years, it was less wrinkled and lined, her features softened and invigorated.

"Inga" I managed to say, you look so different." Inga smiled proudly, "no Amos, it's just that summer has finally arrived." Her comment hardly alleviated my consternation at waking up to find her looking so rejuvenated.

When I managed to get out of bed and groggily make my way downstairs only to find a gaping absence.

"The young girl" I exclaimed, where is she?" Normally she would be stationed by the door on the verandah, gazing out to sea, in deep contemplation or resting. She never went for walks and since the discovery of her pregnancy, my wife had watched over her like a prison guard, never letting her out of her sight, but now she was nowhere to be seen.

Inga shrugged her shoulders, as if she was totally unconcerned.

"She took flight in the night" she said, "probably in search of another household she can sponge off, or perhaps to seek the father of the child, she was a bad sort, we never should have taken her in."

I was amazed at my wife's insouciance, before she'd been over protective to the point of obsessiveness, I just could not imagine such a sudden turn of events, this on top of my dream, which was still resonating in my head. My wife busied herself with various chores and left me lying on the couch recovering. It was market day and she said it would be better if she went alone, saying it would be prudent, in light of my fever. She gathered her things and prepared the horse and cart and set off, telling me she would be back before dark. She was wearing a colorful dress, along with a bonnet, that she'd worn years before at her sister's wedding. People were going to notice this big change in her, they would be just as surprised as I had been. People would gossip no doubt, it was inevitable in such a small town.

Rather than spending time moping about the house I decided to go for a walk along the beach, I would gather some mussels, cockles or whelks at the same time, more for my wife's pleasure, as I was going to have to careful as to my diet, due to this fever. Although it was a warm day, with flies buzzing around the verandah, a strong north easterly breeze kept me cool, as I walked along the sand, which had of intermittent patches of decomposing seaweed, which let out a pungent smell.

As I reached the shoreline, I noticed something lain on the sand that even from far looked a person flat on their back spread eagled looking upwards at the sky. My first thoughts were that it was a piece of driftwood, that uncannily had human shape and form, but as I neared it was obvious I'd chanced upon a cadaver, a woman, with long flowing flaxen hair, it didn't take me long to realize who it was. I arched over held my head in my hands and vomited. It took me a while before I could compose myself and reaffirm my discovery. Her body was naked, and had been sliced open, indeed she looked like she'd been filleted like a fish. What I was looking at was a rigid frame of a body, her insides had all been taken away. A filleting knife had been left next to her, sunlight glinted off its long blade. Surprisingly her body had not been ravaged by any birds or wildlife, it remained perfect, almost sculptural, with this sharp incision, which had been used to extract the baby that had developed in her womb.

I walked back to my house, the horror of what I had seen indelible in my turbulent mind. I had some hours to reflect on it before my wife returned home. I felt nauseous and felt compelled to lie down, on the couch on the verandah. I drifted in and out of consciousness. At one point I even thought I glimpsed a distant figure with long golden hair, dancing to the noise of the ocean, before being engulfed by a thunderous wave.

When I caught sight of my wife maneuvering the horse and cart along the dirt track that lead to our house, I felt a mixture of relief for her return, as well as foreboding, as I had to tell her of my discovery. I called out her name as she dismounted from the cart.

"Amos what is it?" she called back, as I walked closely towards her.

"I discovered a body, the young girl's, dead I tell you."

"Are you sure Amos, perhaps you have been imagining things, you had a raging fever only last night" said my wife in a derisive voice interspersed with laughter, scoffing at my proclamation.

"No really Inga, somebody sliced her right open" I said earnestly. Inga smiled at me like a mother might to make light of a nightmare, after a disturbed child has just woken, "well listen I will go down to the beach and see for myself, you have no doubt let your imagination run wild, you really were poorly last night, I'd have thought you had the common sense to convalesce at home." She sent me a steely look before heading to the beach.

As I waited for her return my own doubts started to creep in. After those vivid dreams I'd had, I believed my mind might be playing tricks on me. My wife seemed to be taking a long time to complete her search, and the longer it seemed to take, the more foolish I felt, for sending her, especially after her solo visit to the market.

When she finally returned she seemed smiling. "Amos I have just walked along the shoreline and all I could find was large monkfish, which had been caught in the nets and obviously thrown back to sea by fishermen, it was a horrible looking thing, but there was no sign of a dead body."

"I am sorry my dear" I replied, "obviously since last night, I haven't been myself."

"Don't worry Amos" said my wife sweetly, "I'll make you some soup, it will do you good."

That night my wife said she needed to do some needle work and feeling still ashamed of myself, I decided to keep out of her way and sat on the verandah, staring out to sea. As time passed a thick mist started to descend. I was about to go inside and prepare for the night, when all of a sudden I heard the sound of men on horseback, dragging clumps of willow branches behind them. Following on behind were two men with Alsatian dogs, with torches burning. The band of men stopped when they reached the shoreline, at the place where I thought I'd seen the dead body. Having dismounted, they seemed to be piling the willow branches into a kind of pyre. Suddenly the dogs yelped in fear and the horses were agitated and began to whinny and break free from those restraining them. Some of the men started to shout and two bolted away in fear. A man who I perceived as the leader hurled the burning torch onto the pyre and another followed suit tossing his into the pyre as flames leapt upwards. The men who had not fled got on their horses and rode in a circle around the pyre.

I called out to my wife, who was concerned with her needlework. She'd come back from the market with white cloth and was cutting them up into small pieces, she was making clothes seemingly for an infant, but why she hadn't divulged and I was fearful of asking her.

"There are men on horseback burning a huge fire" I said with a voice full of concern. She ambled over to the verandah and looked out at the bustle of activity taking place on the shoreline. "Oh it's the mist" she said casually, "a beacon to ward off ships, it's normal in such inclement sailing conditions." In years of living in the house, this had never happened before and it seemed like my wife had for whatever reason had come up with the most absurd fabrication. Why would the men arrive with dogs? Why would they come in such numbers? Why would they be circling the fire, as if they were doing some kind of ritual? Why had some of the men fled in fear?

My wife went back to her needlework. The men continued their circling until the flames started to die down. They left in a line down the beach, like they were a victorious horse parade. I left my wife still doing her needlework and went to bed. As I put my head down on my pillow, I was sure I heard the sound of a shrill scream, a woman in agony, my wife would say it was just a seagull, but I was starting to doubt her explanations and more than this I fearful some strange change had come over her.

It wasn't the kind of change in a person, I would have normally anticipated. It wasn't like she had become disagreeable or loathsome, or more sober, quite the opposite, she seemed more joyful and lighthearted. It was like a new spirit had entered her. But this new spirit unnerved me, because my wife had always been dependable and steadfast, indeed when I introduced her to some of my friends at a party to mark our engagement, it was obvious from their faces, they had marked her down as being rather dull, indeed frumpy. Many had no doubt expected me to marry a more flamboyant woman, instead I'd chosen a woman who was abidingly engrossed in books, a pretty young thing, none the less. It was true she'd developed a few quirks over the years, mostly in our pursuit of a child, but mostly she was the same constant woman I'd married, that was up until now.

This new variant of my wife, seemed to sing songs to herself, the types of songs you might sing to a newborn as well as talking and laughing, always in a soft gentle voice, as if there was an imaginary infant in her arms. I never questioned her, I just observed and took in each new strange occurrence with total amazement.

Though I was afraid of directing my questions to her, concerning the young girl, and what had happened concerning the night riders, I felt a strong urge to find answers elsewhere. When my wife told me she was feeling unwell one morning, on market day, this gave me an opportunity to seek some answers, at the market. Stall holders knew things about the locality, somebody must know something. Perhaps the riders of the night had legendary status. When I asked people if they had anything about a young girl with golden hair, or about a band of men riding horses, I was given either blank looks or sometimes hostile looks. Nobody wanted to divulge any information.

Part Three
"Inside the mind of Jakob Klieberg"

I recalled talk of an old lighthouse keeper, who had a reputation for his knowledge of local history and legends. Many dismissed him as being insane, many would not talk to him, which meant he had adapted into being a great listener, absorbing large amounts of information.

His name was Jakob Klieberg, some said his madness emanated from his long hours spent in a lighthouse. He'd once had two brothers who were lighthouse keepers in the same lighthouse. The brothers were inseparable. Their amity was broken when all three brothers fell in love with the same woman. The youngest brother, decided a long sea journey, would help him ease the burning passion he had for the young girl he'd set his heart on marrying. He joined up with merchant navy and set off around the world, only to succumb to scurvy. The two other brothers returned to their work as lighthouse keepers, but with hours to kill, raging arguments flared up. When it was time for them to be collected, their stint over, only one brother boarded the boat back home.

He claimed his older brother, had taken flight one night and had boarded a Russian ship, destined for Vladivostok. It was a highly unlikely story, many claimed Jakob had murdered his brother, dumping his body in the ocean. He'd proposed to Agnes, shortly after reaching shore, who'd turned down his overtures, saying her love was for Enock, the missing brother.

Jakob had stormed out of her house in a rage. He started drinking heavily. Back on the lighthouse his drinking got worse. Responsible for the night watch, one night as a heavy mist descended, he failed to compete the most fundamental of his duties of illuminating the lighthouse. A fishing boat full of local fishermen had crashed into some rocks, the entire crew had drowned. When it transpired that Jakob had shirked his duties, no doubt due to being totally inebriated, the deaths that occurred that night were totally avoidable, his standing in the community plummeted, soon open hostility towards him became common place, particularly among the wives, who'd lost their husband. He was forced to sit by himself, at the same table at the back of the inn, listening to the conversations of others, a pariah, who had almost become invisible. He always bought two drinks and had a stool at the ready, for the moment his older brother would return, which he claimed would at least restore some of his credibility, but of course his brother never would come back.

It was the fish monger's wife Molly, who'd suggested I seek out Jakob. I'd heard about him a long time before and had vague memories of his father, who was a legendary raconteur. Wherever he went, he had a captive audience listening to his stories and his nighttime venue was the inn, where Jakob went to everyday, without fail. It was little wonder his three sons chose to be lighthouse keepers, with a father such as theirs, they had sought and found solace and tranquility. It was sure that their father had told them story after story of local legends. I'd thought at first Molly was mocking me when she suggested I saw Jakob, when I'd viewed him while going to the market, he seemed as mad as a March hare. Molly told me he would be found in the Fisherman's Arms Inn. One of the few people who showed him any compassion was the Innkeeper, though begrudgingly, as Jakob was a friend of his father and had once saved his father's life following a sailing accident. Jakob didn't bother anyone anyway; he just sat at his table and seemed to melt in with the surroundings.

His appearance was striking, his face ravaged with age, he had long pork chop sideburns that had bushed outwards. His right eye was disproportionate in relation to his drooping left eye, which meant he had a strange fixed expression on his face, like he was permanently confused, or had facial palsy. He had a mass of cysts on his face, made me think of a rock covered in barnacles. Surprisingly he was wearing a double-breasted sack coat; despite the heat of summer.

When I sat down next to him, on the stool reserved for his absent brother, his right eye seemed to protrude even larger. Nobody had so much acknowledged in years, let alone talked to him. "May I talk to you?" I asked nervously. He didn't answer me, perhaps he was still stunned at my sudden appearance at his table, he just cocked his head upwards, and nodded, that large right eye fixed on me.

Slowly I began to recount my story, starting with the young girl arriving on the beach. His right eye seemed to flicker, and his face formed a twisted expression, when I talked of the horse riders. When I had finally finished, he burst into hysterical laughter. Heads turned, conversations were cut dead.

I thought to myself Molly had sent me, for her own amusement, the man just seemed barking mad. I felt foolish having wasted my time and energy in chronicling my story. When Jakob's laughter subsided, he peered at me with a more sober face.
"I suppose you should come back to mine, the locals around here don't take kindly to such stories being bandied about."

I followed him slowly behind, people staring at me, as we passed them. I suppose I was the first person to enter his house in years.

His house was small but stacked full of objects of one kind or another. There were lobster pots, fishing nets, fishing rods that were obviously broken, oars for rowing boats, life buoys, ropes, pairs of fisherman's boots, and fisherman's oilskins. There was a huge collection of seashells, he'd obviously gathered over the years, on lonely walks along the beach. There were bird's skulls and skeletons. There were piles of dust covered books, piled one on top of the other, looking like towers that might topple over at any moment. There were old newspapers, tied in bundles that had yellowed so badly, their content would surely be illegible. It was natural that wish such an array of old objects linked to the sea, there would be quite a profound odor. Indeed it took me time to acclimatize, to Jakob's unusual habitat. With a forced smile Jakob said, "find a space that is if you can find one." After shuffling some clothes and papers about I found some space on a sofa, which had chunks of horsehair protruding out its frayed covers. Jakob took out a clay pipe and stuffed some tobacco from a pouch. The smoke the pipe emitted a sweet woody aroma, which helped to nullify some of the more noxious odors that had prevailed before.

After a couple of intakes of smoke, Jakob suddenly began to speak. "I knew she would come at some point," he mused, his head tilted resting in the palm of one hand, while the other handheld his pipe, which moved freely from side to side, as if he was gently conducting an invisible orchestra.

 "She, you mean Astrid?" I enquired softly.

"Yes," he replied, his right eye twitching, his lazy left almost shut.

"Tell me about her," I demanded, "I only know her through voices in my head."

"We have to go back a long way in time" said Jakob with a sigh, "back to a time when this country was great, ruled by a powerful king." Astrid was his youngest daughter, the most beautiful of his five daughters, his favorite child, but with an erratic flamboyant personality that even this strong King could not reign in. The King wanted his influence in foreign lands to grow further afield and his distant cousin, the King in a southern realm, had a son who was of an age when a wife was a requirement. The only problem was, this son was far from handsome, indeed his only real credentials were his royal parentage. The King of this southern realm commissioned the country's greatest poet and scribe to draft some love letters to Astrid, which his son, who had neither writing skills nor romantic notions, copied with his scrawled handwriting.

The country's greatest draughtsman was commissioned to do a drawing of the prince in all his regal robes and splendor. This with the proviso that the work flattered the young prince, emphasizing his princely looks, rather than his unfortunate imperfections, of which there were many including a bent nose, piggy eyes and a decidedly pointed chin. His shoulders and legs were of uneven height, but the draughtsman against his better judgment, made alterations to accommodate the King's wishes. The final draught bore little resemblance, to the prince, but the King paid him none the less and sent the misleading fabricated image on its way to Astrid.

When the two finally met, Astrid's disappointment was evident; she was in no hurry to marry anyway, feeling her life required a few adventures, before the more sober duties of regal life took hold. Her father spent weeks trying to convince her to cement the marriage, firstly with forceful words, which proved fruitless. His second measure was to try to coax her with gifts and more gentle words. Of course, she accepted his gifts, but it was obvious she had little intention to acquiesce to her father's wishes. When her father told her, she was now to be betrothed to a particularly sadistic nobleman of seventy-five years old and would be whipped within an inch of her life if she didn't accept, the young prince seemed the more acceptable of the two. Reluctantly she set off with an entourage including a band of men on horseback to guard her, as well as sizeable dowry, which included gold coins, silver and gold ingots, gems including opals, sapphires and emeralds.

The entourage was to travel by the coastal road. One evening they arrived at a small fishing village, where a man by the coastline was holding an audience to an enthusiastic crowd. Against the better judgment of those responsible for the care of the princess, she ordered the entourage to stop. She said she wanted to take in the words of the man, who was a mestare (master). He was on the shoreline, as the tide was coming in. His left hand held a blue lapis stone, with darker and lighter blue markings on it. His right arm held a boy, of about six years old, his limbs looked weak and feeble, his legs had wooden braces on them, obviously he had been struck down by terrible affliction. The Master held the boy up to sky, where the stars were formed like the mouth of a wolf. He seemed to grip the stone ever stronger in the palm of his hand and seemed to be summoning some kind of inner force. There was silence as well as a palpable tension among the sizable crowd.

The master mumbled some words to himself and then suddenly let out an almighty scream, as if releasing some energy. Once the scream which could easy be heard in the next village, such was its fortitude, had subsided, he placed the boy, so his legs were covered by an incoming wave. He walked away from the incoming sea and placed the boy on the sand, releasing him from his wooden braces.

'Now stand up boy and walk' he commanded. The boy looked up at him, at first fearful he would be unable to fulfill master's request. The eyes of the crowd were now fixed on the little boy. He used his arms to shift himself upwards, before putting any weight on his spindly legs. His first step saw him tumbling down on the sand. The crowd groaned and held their breath as he attempted a second step, which again ended with him slumped on the ground. The crowd was starting to believe, the master had failed, when the little boy using all of his concentration and remaining energy managed to complete his first step. The crowd roared.

The Master remained unmoved, as if he'd just completed a menial task. This first significant step forward, encouraged the boy to attempt more steps. Cautiously he walked towards his father, who picked him up and said, 'the master has cured my boy, he can walk'. The princess looked on in awe. She was soon ordering her entourage to set up camp close to the beach, they were not moving on, that was for sure, despite protests from those who were responsible for her. They were powerless because the King had heard of an uprising in a Northern Province. He would quell this insurrection and would then make his way down, along with other key dignitaries to join the wedding festivities.

Now the whimsical princess was throwing all those carefully laid plans into disarray by insisting on meeting The Master, who happened to live in a modest house that looked out onto the bay. The Master was quite a shy unassuming man, who happened to have these powers of healing. He lived by himself and lived quite a simple life, fishing from the rocks, reading and spending time in deep contemplation. The princess sent one of her entourage to see the Master, to arrange an audience with him. Most men would have been flattered to have interest in them from a beautiful young princess, but the Master had seen this demand as an imposition, he had other things to do, but reluctantly agreed. She had arrived at his house, wearing some of her finest attire and despite being on the road for a number of days, she managed to look fresh and alluring. Conversation with Master had proved awkward. Of course, she had commenced with flattery, saying how impressed she was by his miracle. The Master had shrugged and had continued staring out to sea, avoiding her stare that was relentlessly fixed on him.

He showed no interest in her life, nor the reason why she was travelling. One thing was certain she was falling in love with him. He had slightly wavy long fair hair and a well-kept beard, his face rather long and with a broad, straight forehead. His eyes were blue and hypnotic, his nose was straight with a prominent bridge, his cheeks were large and slightly protruding. Tallish, with a perfectly proportioned physique, lithe and harmonious, the princess found the Master, thoroughly appealing. With men usually laying themselves at her feet, the princess found it hard to digest here was a man who seemed to show no interest in her, she found it impossible to penetrate his cold demeanor. She left feeling deflated, of course he hadn't been impolite, he'd been more curt and disinterested. In a way this rejection only stirred up stronger feelings to the Master, as well as a stronger determination to win his heart.

An argument flared up; when she decreed the entourage were to stay a further night, if not longer. This meant the journey down south would further delayed, any more delays would mean they would be late for a state wedding. The King would be furious, not only with his daughter, but also with those who'd been so liberal in allowing her to pander to her whims.

It was late at night and the Princess taking a stroll along the beach, while pondering how she could gain the master's love, noticed that lights were still burning in humble home. She walked towards his house, hoping he wouldn't be angered by her intrusion. She had a light robe on and suddenly she had the urge to take it off, to feel the light sea breeze settle on her body. Feeling giddy with emotion, she suddenly felt also like she wanted to dance. She gambled that he would be more impressed by her naked body as well as a sultry dance, than he had by her conversation. She wanted to come slowly into his eyeshot, a sudden surprise on a moonlit night.

He seemed engrossed in a book, rapt in thought, lain on the verandah. She started her dance, and was soon in a trance, absorbed by the dance and its ever evolving flowing movements, but still the master's eyes were fixed rigidly on the book. When a fly suddenly disturbed him and flicked it away with his hand, he caught sight of her for the first time. Rather than being disturbed by this sudden imposition to his evening of contemplation and enlightenment, he was compelled to watch and was soon absorbed and in awe of not only the dance but the naked dancer. The dance continued for a long time, and the Master just looked on, hardly drawing in breath, totally transfixed as the dance seemed to gather momentum. Finally she stopped, having flexed every sinew of her body, driving herself to do movements, she never imagined herself capable of. There was a fraught silence between them.

Suddenly the Master beckoned her to join him on the verandah. She stood unabashed naked in front of him, as if offering herself.

"That was most enchanting" he said in a soft voice, as she smiled down at him.
"You must be tired after such exertion" he said, his eyes feasting on her naked body.
"The night is not over Master" she replied, "we should take advantage of such a beautiful night as this."

The Master had never before experienced a woman such as the princess, no woman had dared get close to him, because he had an aura about him. In a way because of mystical powers, it seemed inappropriate, perhaps his powers might be corrupted, by physical contact. This did not stop the young princess, she could tell by his looks, he wanted her. They spent the night together on the verandah. As dawn broke, there was sudden realization in the camp that the princess was not in her tent. One of her female attendants had seen her wander on the beach, but assumed she was just cooling her feet in the sea water and would wander quickly back. Men were quickly dispatched to search for her, but she was nowhere to be found.

Suddenly she was spotted, surprisingly leaving the house of the man known as the Master.
'Are you alright princess, you haven't been deflowered have you?' demanded the leader of the entourage. 'No everything is fine, I'm in love can't you see.'

'Of course you are princess you are on your way to your wedding.'
The princess was walking on air, replied 'no I'm never going to leave this place, and there will be no such wedding, my heart now belongs to the Master and always will.' This remark sent a shockwave through the entourage. They had hardly completed a fifth of their journey and yet it had come to a grinding halt, the King would punish them severely. There was one positive to be had from this sorry story, notably the dowry, which they could all profit from, after all the princess was not going to need it, if she was to spend her life with a humble mystic, who lived off the fruits of sea, in a stark home. The temptation proved too much.

However a watertight story had to be contrived, a story strong enough to convince the King. The blame for this outrage was placed on the shoulders of the villagers and indeed the Master. The villagers, they would later claim were in league with some unscrupulous pirates had ambushed and abducted the princess, who was now confined in the master's house. The dowry was now on a ship that had sailed far out to sea. A story also had to be put into place for the princess. A meeting had been held, while the princess slept, having failed to capture any sleep the night before. They told her that she should follow where her heart was taking her. She would have to make her peace with the King one day in the future, but they swore on oath, they would not reveal her whereabouts. They also said they would bury the dowry, that it would be hers when she needed it. Being so in love and buoyant she was naïve enough to believe them. She watched them bury the chest by a tree, that had been struck by lightning, on the hill that overlooked the bay, then watched them ride off. She returned to the Master, thinking her life had now turned a new and exciting direction, away from her oppressive father and the routine of court life.

The villagers noted a change in the Master, that aloofness that characterized him, seemed to have lifted, as he smiled and acknowledged them. Of course he'd lived amongst them for a long time, but in a way he was living in another dimension far from most mortals.

Naturally they were suspicious of the princess, had she beguiled the Master? Perhaps he was less fallible than they'd imagined. Why was she now residing in a simple house, when she could be living in the grandeur of a palace? Wasn't she on her way to marry a prince in some foreign land? The more they thought about this new situation, the more wary they became. Some even said the Master had married the young girl, in a secret ceremony on the beach.

Their fears were not without foundation, when in the middle of the night men on horseback arrived with torches, burning to the ground every house, except the Master's. In fact, this exception had gone against the King's decree. They had also been ordered to bring the Master back with them to face a trial for treason. However, face to face with the man, they were loathed to destroy his home and take him with them, being fearful of his powers, of which they had told exaggerated stories. If he could make a cripple walk, he could also conjure up terrible maledictions blighting their families and children for generations to come. In fact, he gave them no reason to fear him. He had been sad and philosophical about handing over the princess, but never said a harsh word or lifted his hand in anger.

The cost to the village was catastrophic, their punishment emphatic. One of the entourage had talked and when the King returned from repressing the northern uprising and discovered that his daughter was no longer en route and that rumor had it she was now ensconced with some mystic, he ruthlessly went about punishing those responsible, using the most clinical and sadistic torture techniques known to man. The dowry he suspected would never be recuperated, but his wayward daughter would and for good measure the village would be wiped off the map, by a band of his most elite and coldblooded soldiers.

The Master did not live long after this momentous event. He lived as a hermit. He

was a broken man, his soul in torment. He tried
to purge the memory of the princess out of his
mind. He'd let her go to the soldiers, without a
struggle and he didn't have it within him to go
and search for her. She'd shouted to him that she
would return, but he didn't really have faith in
the promise, she could never escape the clutches
of the King. Equally it was the deaths of the
villagers that affected him greatly. Living in
isolation he had time to brood over what had
happened and awful thoughts entered his head,
that perhaps he'd been enchanted by a sorceress,
who for a short time had corrupted his mind,
body and soul. Putting his life in context he
realized despite for all his good deeds in his life,
his life was now tainted with blood on his hands.
After days moping on the rocks, staring out to
sea, some said he walked into the sea, until
submerged by giant incoming waves and was
taken into the heart of the ocean. In fact, there
was no evidence of him dying or the way in
which he died.

If the princess had been touched by the
master's goodness, this was not in evidence by
the time she reached the King's palace in
disgrace, her bitterness and resentment, knew no
bounds. There was also some diplomatic
patching up to do. Having no other daughters to
dispatch, the King was in an awkward position,
he had a young niece, but she was only ten years
old, quite far off marrying age. In fact, the

princess' non arrival had been taken very badly, as an insult. There were calls for war against the country responsible for such an insult. No war ever started, however other stark reprisals were put in place.

The countries most notorious sorceress was engaged to place the most powerful curse on the young princess. If she ever gave birth, she would die giving birth and the infant would be born the son of the devil. Trading contracts were torn up and plans for both countries to go on a mutually beneficial voyage of discovery around the unexplored parts of the world, were shelved. The non-marriage proved costly for the King and soon uprisings that had started in the north, began to spread down south. His capricious daughter was almost held a prisoner.

Bitter about her abduction and now incarceration, her heart still ached to be reunited with the Master, she managed without her father's consent to consult a seer. The seer confirmed the curse had been put upon her. The seer foretold that the princess would never meet the Master, in his present lifetime, it would take time, perhaps some centuries before the princess could once again reunite with the Master. The Master would be reincarnated, it was ordained, but the princess would have to wait for such a time, depending on the phase of the moon. The seer said she would provide a chart, mapping her future as well as the Masters'.

The seer said the curse could never be lifted, but she knew of some spells that meant the Princess could be reborn at the anointed time. From the time of her death to her rebirth, the princess would reside in the Otherworld, a realm or realms it is said that exist beyond the reach of the physical senses, but which are nevertheless real.

The seer said the Master in the future would be changed, she would find that he had a wife. This wife would be unable to bare children. This wife should not be seen as an impediment, indeed she could be exploited. If the princess couldn't bring a child into the world, then a surrogate would prove to be a big asset.

The princess was not held captive much longer, the details of her passing away was shrouded in mystery. After spells had been placed on her, some said she died, from unknown causes. Some said she was pregnant, when she died. Some said the King had poisoned her, having never forgiven her. His power and credibility were waning, if couldn't control his daughter, how could he rule over a kingdom? The more likely truth was that she was smuggled out of her place of incarceration, and was buried in the countries deepest glacier, to lie dormant until one day she would reawaken.

With the moon passing through the phase the seer had foretold, she was reborn at the predestined time and has been amongst us in recent times, fully conscious of her previous life and in the same physical state as her earlier incarnation, still with an unborn child. A life which was incomplete, as she had to return to the Master, who she knew had been reincarnated and was residing in the same abode by the sea. In her new life, she had few resources, but she imagined that buried by a tree there was the chest, which contained her dowry. She gained a reputation as a great dancer, in a town in a northern province. She refused all the advances of men, saying she was taken. Nobody knew who she was, where she'd come from, she had simply just appeared from nowhere.

She saved up some money before travelling south. On her journey, she met a band of hardened mercenaries back from a war. They were travelling along the same coastal route. She asked if she could accompany them, thinking she would be safer traveling through some of the more dangerous terrain, where wolves prowled at night and outlaws preyed on the vulnerable.

They thought it amusing to travel with this lone woman, indeed a beautiful one at that. Of course, they expected some kind of reward for protecting her. She had no resources, except the dowry, which she imagined had remained untouched over the centuries. It was the only thing she had to offer.

One night one of the mercenaries, called Joel Berg had the most terrible fever. He'd sustained a leg injury and the wound had neither healed nor been cleansed. If nothing was done, he would surely die. The other mercenaries were resigned to him dying, but out of desperation they asked the young girl, they had picked up on their travels, if she might know of a way to help him, in his hour of need. She'd learnt things in her short time with the master and the seer had also imparted her wisdom, mostly of a darker nature. Holding strongly in the palm of her hand, a blue lapis stone, one of her few possessions, she forced the raging fever out. Using Sphagnum moss, she dressed the wound. The mercenaries were in awe of the sudden transformation they saw in the sick man.

Building a fire later that night, she had danced, while one of the men Tor Stranz, played the fiddle. She thought she had won the favor of the men and had compensated for their protection by charming and entertaining them, as well as for saving the life of Joel Berg. Unfortunately, the men were not swayed by these contributions, they only traded in money.
They planned to sell the young girl once they had arrived at a port, they imagined they would get a good price from a foreign buyer, looking for a beautiful whore. Her dance had also managed to stir other emotions, primarily lust. Thor was the first one to try to enter her tent, as she slept. Her talon like fingers gauged his eyes, as she fought him off like wild cat protecting its prey.

Later that night, Dag Flom, a veteran soldier of many campaigns, was also warded off, while sustaining a vicious scratch down the side of his face. The next morning the mercenaries couldn't understand how Thor and Dag, had come by injuries such as these away from the field of battle and during the night. The two men were afraid to tell the truth. Equally they were afraid of the she devil, they had foolishly tried to seduce.

It did not take long before the men started to realize they had in their midst, a dangerous woman. Feeling this strong antipathy towards her, while eating cod fish soup, round a fire, that crackled and hissed, with sparks wafting upwards, a cluster of stars looming above, as the men talked in soft voices, excluding her from the conversation, she suddenly blurted out, 'where we are going I know of a huge stash of precious stones, ingots, riches enough, to keep you in spender for the rest of your lives.' At first the men scoffed, but as time passed their intrigue got the better of them. She was such a mystifying woman, even something that sounded wildly implausible and fantastical, could turn out to be true.

They were still a few days away from the place she said the stash would be found. At night she felt safer in her tent, none of the other men tried to enter, and if they had she

would have stabbed them with a knife one of the
men had carelessly left around.

As the party neared her final destination the
moment of truth had arrived. The tree was still
there, its spindly branches were extremely
eroded, with sharp grooves running through
them.

The young girl pointed to the spot, where she still
maintained they would find the stash. They
started like hungry dogs round a carcass to
exhume what was allegedly buried underneath.
When Dag scratched away at what appeared to
be a chest of some description, the men's spirits
lifted, while the credibility of the young girl's
claim also seemed stronger.

It was when they winched open the lid, to find a
mound of sand, some rocks and a few tarnished
silver coins, providing evidence that there had
been a stash, their previous jubilation turned to
raging anger.

All eyes settled on the young girl, who
reached for the knife and screamed 'touch me
and I'll make you bleed'. Two men among the
party believed her, the others jeered. The young
girl suddenly took flight, running in the darkness.
Of course she was helpless against twelve men,
but running towards the place where the Master
resided, gave her hope, perhaps he would prove
her salvation. When she entrapped by a net one
of the mercenaries threw over her, any residing
hopes diminished. What they did next was

brutal. They tore off her clothes, until she was fully naked. They attached a rope round her neck, which Dag attached to his saddle. She was forced to run along the beach, first at a gentle pace, then at a quicker pace. Some of the men carried torches. The empty chest had proved a bitter blow, so now they wanted a bit high jinx, but not to kill her, as they thought she could fetch a good price. The young girl stumbled but was able to get back on her feet. She seemed to show a remarkable resilience, her spirit not easily broken.

Dag suddenly lost control of his horse which bolted forward, sending the young girl sprawling to the ground. He managed to regain control. The young girl lay flat on her face on the wet sand. 'She's dead' said Joel, 'she's either been strangled or her neck is broken, nobody could survive being dragged like that.' Dag untied the rope around her neck, her body remained motionless. 'She's not breathing' said Dag, dropping her head face down in the sand. The men rode off, leaving the young girl for dead."

After talking rapidly, almost without pausing for breath, Jakob suddenly stopped and let out a long sigh. He looked at me full in the face and said, "the rest of the story you surely know." Before I could answer he began to laugh, a long ceaseless cackle, tears streaming down his face.

Once his laugh had finally abated, I had one more question, I needed to satisfy for myself. "There were some riders and men with dogs, the other night, who might they be."
"Well," he said, "these men are not like the mercenaries, they are religious men," "You see when they got to port, one of the mercenaries began to talk of a she devil, word reached some church elders, and a party of men were dispatched to find out if there was any truth in this. When they arrived all they found was a hollowed out body of a young woman, who they suspected was previously with child. Though they had found a cadaver, they were still fearful and thought it best to dispose of the body by burning it with branches, they had brought with them should the necessity arise.

The story is not over is it, as I am sure you realize, there's only one woman who can act as the surrogate for the child, we both know who that is." His laugh echoed around the room even stronger. Suddenly Jakob lurched forward, his breathing sounding labored, with a rattling sound emanating from his lungs. His head lolled forward, like a chicken with a broken neck. He was dying in front of me, but in effect he'd been dead for years.

I left his house, with no concern for a dying man, but more deeply perturbed by the story I'd been told. I'd discovered a new facet of myself, that of my previous incarnation. I had been tracked down by a person from my previous incarnation, who had wished to reunite with me. Of course, I had listened to a man who was the son of a famous raconteur, a man that was blatantly deranged. However, a lot of what he said seemed to really correlate with my recent experiences, as unbelievable as this might seem.

I had completely lost track of time, as I walked to my horse and cart, dusk was clearly setting in, the light languid and shadowy. I would have to lie to my wife, I thought of saying one of the horses became lame, a nasty thorn having lodged in its hoof.

When I finally got home, I found her on the verandah; she was more concerned with what she was doing, rather than my absence. She was making a straw doll and seemed so absorbed, I felt like I was an intruder. I mumbled my excuse, and all she did was give me a look of mild amusement, as if I'd just recounted a funny anecdote. I felt disturbed by her apparent indifference. The doll was not the only one of her endeavors, draped over the chair was a maternity smock. Some of the Jakob's words reentered my head, *there's only one woman who can act as the surrogate for the child, we both know who that is* but I was loathed to question her, her answers might prove too hard to bear.

She managed to disengage herself from her doll and we had some soup together, while hardly uttering one word to one another. I was feeling more and more estranged. The night would prove to be long and hard. She couldn't seem to settle, finding it impossible to find a comfortable position, also I noticed her breath was particularly sour. I managed to drop off, but woke up, my wife was gently snoring. Through the dingy light I noticed the image of a face suddenly materialize in the mirror, which was directly in front of our marital bed. The image in the mirror started to sharpen and I began to realize it was Jakob's old and wizened face, staring at me with a fixed malevolent grin on his face. I buried my head in my pillow, trying to block out, this disturbing image, while fearful my wife might awaken. When I had sufficient courage to look at the mirror again, his vision had gone.

As I started to become more alert, I began to dismiss this vision as a mere lapse of my overburdened mind. Moreover, as my mind returned to Jakob's story it seemed more and more ludicrous. A story about a princess seemed more folklore, than any genuine bearing on my life. I certainly didn't feel like I was a reincarnation of "this master" he talked about. Anything that had rang true was due to wild coincidences and that he was simply an over-imaginative anecdotist, like his renowned father, who had long gone insane, after a traumatic life, a portion of which he'd spent as an outcast.

Part four
"The feast"

After my strange encounter with Jakob, after
spending the night tossing and turning, my mind
troubled, I managed to slip into a deep sleep.
When I finally woke up, to my surprise I realized
my wife was no longer at my side. I hauled
myself out of bed and lumbered downstairs,
expecting to see my wife, however she was
nowhere in the house nor in the back garden. I
called her name but there was no response. I
went onto the verandah, while looking out across
the bay, I saw a distant figure, with a spade,
digging away close to the rocks. I watched until
she pulled something out the ground; put it under
her arm while holding the spade with other,
before purposely walking back to our house. I
could not imagine what had possessed her to
leave the house for such a deed nor imagine the
contents of whatever she had retrieved. I
pretended I had not been witness to her morning
sortie. She seemed to have a look of contentment
on her face, as if she'd accomplished something
wonderful. I pretended to be immersed with the
food I was preparing to eat, as I peeled an apple
she placed a metal box that had obviously rusted
and degraded but which was still in a good

enough condition to conceal and preserve whatever lay within, by the alter.

She offered no explanation; she just asked me if I had slept well, which of course I hadn't. We went about our separate errands; everything seemed to be like a normal regular day, until I heard the sound of a young kid goat squealing. The noise was horrendous. My wife had a crazed look on her face as she cut through the jugular vein with a sharp knife. She hung the head of the kid downwards so as to thoroughly drain the blood. My mind was filled with shock but was also tinged with anger. We had not discussed slaughtering a goat. When it came to slaughtering goats, it was usually my thankless task. My wife loved and tendered our small herd of goats and usually would only agree to a slaughtering after much insistence on my part and would cry relentlessly after its demise. "What have you done?" I demanded as blood continued to trickle from the slayed goat, indeed her favorite she'd named affectionately "Lif". "We are going to have a feast Amos" said my wife triumphantly, "it's the day of Samhain and we are going to gather all we can to celebrate it." This seemed surprising to me, as we had only ever really celebrated our birthdays, as well as the passing of a year. I knew Samhain to be the time when the curtain between the worlds is at its thinnest point. The mystical doorway between dimensions being more accessible, so the dead could be reincarnated and pass through it. I couldn't fathom her reason to feast, nobody from our families had died recently.

I was told I should go and get some potatoes, peas, cabbage and carrots. My wife busied herself skinning the goat, removing its internal organs, then cutting up the carcass, seasoning it with fresh rosemary. At midday, we ate a light lunch, a soup with meatballs. As my wife cleaned the bowls, she said she had tasks to do and suggested I went for a walk. The idea appealed as lunch had been conducted in a strange atmosphere, hardly a word exchanged, perhaps we were both fearful of what might be said.

I set off for the beach, the tide was coming in, the sea was dark and turbulent, the sky was equally gray and ominous as foreboding as the night I imagined lay before me. My walk on the beach did nothing to appease my fears. Recalling my wife's earlier visit to the beach, I had an urge to rummage around the vicinity searching for any indications of her intent. The beach did not offer too many clues, the sea had seen to this. There were caves nearby, the perfect place to hide a corpse or go about some malicious deed. I still craved for her whereabouts of the missing young girl. The caves proved equally fruitless. Sea Rats disturbed by my entrance scurried about a decimated seemingly headless sea lion like creature. Some seagulls had also taken their portion of the hapless creature, while flies hovered, in close proximity.

The image made me feel nauseous, I quickly averted my eyes, and clambered out the cave. Normally a visit to the caves brought me untold pleasure, the caves being a trove of riches, but this visit had proved abhorrent. I trudged back to the house, feeling increasingly apprehensive. What did my wife have in mind, with this celebration?

When I approached the door I heard the sound of a woman moaning in agony. While on the table there lay a wonderful lavish feast, on the floor my wife was writhing in agony.
"You have returned" she managed to say.

A steady flow of blood had caused her white dress to have massive scarlet rivulet. I ran for a towel to stem the flow of blood, but too my horror discovered a fetus head lodged between her legs. Its eyes looked at me imploringly. I fought hard to retain my self-control. My impulse was to run out of the house, leaving my wife in her desperate situation, releasing myself from having to view this abomination that lay before me.

My wife was more and more desperate. I began to hear those voices in my head, Astrid was present, back to the fore, on reflection she had been present a long time, my

wife as I had known her had departed a long time ago. Astrid had resided in my wife's body.
"*Master, Master, you have to save us,*" pleaded the voice in my head.
"But I am not The Master" I shouted out loud, anger welling up.
"*Take the drink on the table*" implored the voice. I looked at the table, the feast had indeed been well prepared, incense burnt, there was savory pumpkin soup, a massive meat pie, Colcannon, bread of the dead as well as other food that she had never prepared before. There was a knife she had used to slay the goat. Then there was the chalice, she was obviously referring to.

My mind was now sharply divided into different parts. Should I save my wife, by transforming myself into the Master, by bringing back his soul or should I follow my instinct and walk away or perhaps even put an end to this woman purporting to be my wife. Time was running out.

While my mind was in this horrific quandary, I heard the sound of men on horses approaching at rapid speed. One of the men dismounted and ran to the entrance of my house. "Don't listen to this she-devil," commanded the man. I dared look at the man for a few brief moments. He was dressed head to toe in brilliant white, his face shrouded by a mask. Around his neck swung a sturdy wooden cross. This new intervention only augmented my distress.

"Kill her, I say!" said the man pointing a finger at my possessed wife.

"I can't" I said feebly.

"Don't let your fragility, get in the way of God's deeds," said the man menacingly.

Suddenly the fetus let out this excruciating piercing screech. I couldn't stand it, I grabbed the knife on the table and jabbed many times at my wife, to stop the sound emanating from the fetus. The screech seemed to continue however, interminably. I couldn't stand it, I ran out of the house, still with knife in hand. My head was in turmoil, I had just killed my wife.

I heard a frail voice in my head, almost a whisper… *"how could you Master"*.

I shouted out loud "I'm no Master, I'm just a murderer!"

Tears streamed down my face. Through my blurry vision I saw the men on horseback throw their torches at my house. Fire soon billowed out the house.

Then there was one long shrill scream from the fetus, a sound that resonated in my head.

I was still deep in my torment, when suddenly one of the men who'd arrived on horseback hit me on the back of the head with a wooden club. I am not sure how long I remained unconscious, my head lain on a support of sea urchins.

When I became conscious, I was totally alone, just me and the vast expanse of the beach. The tide was out and I heard the high-pitched rasping squeals of seagulls, flying overhead. My head still throbbed and as time passed, fleeting memories of the night before started entering my mind causing sharp pangs of anguish. Obviously, the men on horseback had long parted. With a lot of effort, I managed to haul myself up. The sun beamed down, the sky was a perfect blue, like the kind of day after a passing of a storm.

I walked laboriously up the beach to the house, imagining the damage to be devastating. In a way, I rather hoped that it had been destroyed, it would help close a dark and disturbing chapter in my life. Part of me cautioned not to go into the blackened remains of the house. I could head towards the city, start a new life, and try to eradicate from my mind what had gone on, over time. It seemed a much easier option. But then equally I had this urge to enter my home, for cathartic reasons, to purge my conscience, perhaps I should do the decent thing and bury my wife, she deserved at least this.

Light burst through the windows, illuminating all, I could hardly bare to look, for the horrors my eyes might uncover. There was no sign of my wife's body, I expected to see the charred remains. Perhaps the men on horseback had dragged her away. The fire had not done as much damage as I had expected. The walls were blackened but the structure had remained solid and the ceiling had not fallen down. I began to doubt some of my memories from the night before, after all it had all happened so quickly and I had received a severe blow to the back of my head.

The house had a vacant feeling about it, as if its soul had been sucked out, it was like I was visiting a place I hadn't visited in a long time, I was rediscovering my own home. A chalice glinted in the sunlight. Strange objects surrounded the chalice, that gave me the impression they were part of some black arts ritual. My wife would never have dabbled with such things, she was a spiritual person, who believed in goodness. She was not a regular church goer, but I often chanced upon her praying.

On the other hand, Astrid definitely had an ethereal side to her, she had managed to captivate me, but at the same time I was daunted by her. She had severely ruffled the mundane life I had led, especially with those wild proclamations and her propensity to be able to enter my head. All that talk of me being some kind of reincarnation of a "Master" filled me with fear.

While deep in thought, my solitude was broken by a sound. With more concentration, I was able to make out the sound of a baby fighting for breath. The sound emanated from under a cloth, by the table where the feast had

been laid out. I edged warily over to the cloth. I
bent over and pulled the cloth from the wheezing
baby. My eyes set on a horribly disfigured face,
skin gnarled, leathery and charred looking. I felt
immediate revulsion, but in equal part I felt a
sudden surge of pity for vulnerable infant.
Suddenly a voice in my head, childlike,
imploring began to build up, as if working
towards a crescendo.
"Drink from the chalice!"
"Drink from the chalice!"
"Drink from the chalice!"
I felt like I had lost control of my body and mind.
I found myself maneuvering towards the chalice,
my hand reaching to clutch it with both hands. I
lifted it towards my mouth and drank the
contents. Its contents tasted sweet, like a
combination of oranges, coconut and pineapple. I
felt like I was being drawn into a large vortex
rotating at speed. I, Amos Toft, seemed to be
dissolving away into obscurity, while a new force
was taking over.

Part five

The Master returns to his rightful abode

Amos Toft was an irrelevance. He resided in my house, a momentary imposter, but I am the true custodian. He is banished and I have taken over his body. I am back among the living where I should always be. It is true his departure meant the child could be saved. After the transition of souls had been completed I took the stricken child in my arms and carried him outside. It would take all my mental faculties to get the infant well again, as it had the previous night to ward off the men who had dared to enter my domain. I took a clump of sea kelp and pressed it to the infants face. I looked to the sky and recited an incantation. Slowly I took away the kelp from the child's face. It was as I expected. The newborn was now blessed with perfect skin. More than this he was a child of perfect beauty.

He was of course born out of my love for Astrid, the young woman who had beguiled me, our mutual love will carry on through the centuries. I made it my lifelong duty to bring the child up. He would always be in perfect health, of pure mind. I would keep him well a far from the outside world. When of age, I would teach

him of his origins and of matters to do with
spirituality.

As he grew up, he was a delightful
child. I did not refer to his mother, his world
revolved around me and me alone. I kept an
unflinching fixated eye on the child, if anyone
approached my house I would quickly escort him
inside, away from any intruders. He was so
precious to me, my one source of joy and would
let nobody or nothing come between us.

I called my son Aksel. He had
piercing blue eyes and blond curls.
When he had reached a suitable age, I cleared a
space in my house, which would act as a school
room. I had sufficient books, as well as deep
source of knowledge myself. The boy quickly
took to his lessons and had a curious inquiring
mind. Equally he grew physically strong, a
powerful swimmer. He always helped me with
jobs around the house, chopping logs, repairing
walls and fences. As he developed, at the same
time, I also felt that I was aging. I was the
incumbent in Amos Toft's body and physically he
was no longer a young man.

One day I was walking along
the beach with Aksel. Suddenly Aksel stopped
and said, "look Father".
I looked down to see a man spread-eagled, on the
beach.
"What's wrong with him"? demanded Aksel,
who was obviously fascinated. The man had

obviously drunk too much, he was a traveler by looks of things, he had stumbled and fallen, hitting a rock.

"I can help the man" I said confidently. The wound looked deep, but the man was still breathing.

"Go back to the house" I ordered Aksel.

"But I want to stay" insisted Aksel.

The boy of course was totally naïve and innocent concerning mortality and the frailty of human life.

I let him stay, boldly saying again I would cure him, he stood a few paces back as I tried to revive the man. My left hand held a blue lapis stone, I looked to the skies and under my breath recited an incantation. I expected the man's breathing to get stronger, but this was not the case, indeed it seemed his breath was now even shallower. I tried more assiduity. I tried to communicate with Eir, to see if she could intercede on my behalf. Again, my efforts fell short.

The man was clearly dying and all my efforts were falling desperately short. His pulse was growing weaker. Suddenly he let out a gentle sigh and his body went limp, he was dead. I felt crestfallen.

I was The Master, wasn't I?

Or was I still Amos Toft, this thought horrified me. I reassured myself by reminding myself I had revived the boy, something only the Master could do, also I had managed to expel the soul of Amos Toft, it is I the Master who inhabits his body. *Why had the powers invested in me, failed me?* Did I have boundaries to my powers? Aksel latched on to my despair.

"What's the matter Father"?

"Go back to the house, like I told you" I snapped. Aksel walked solemnly back to the house, while collected my thoughts. The boy knew nothing of death, he was barely conscious of different maladies. How was I going to explain this episode? Equally he knew nothing of alcohol.

I went to the work shed, grabbed a shovel to begin the process of burying the man, dragging him to a remote spot. He was a stranger who had intruded on me and my son's ideal solitude. I wanted his memory to quickly banished. Having dumped his body in the ground, I quickly set about covering it up.

My next task was to face my son, to give him explanations. I found Aksel in his bedroom, his back turned to me, looking out to sea.

"What happened to the man?" Aksel demanded, obviously in a state of shock and confusion.

"He died Aksel, I tried to revive him, but he died." I spoke in a mournful voice, shaking my head.

"Died…what's that?" the youngster demanded.

"He is no longer alive, he has stopped breathing, his life is over" I said in desperation, realizing explaining death to a child who had no notion of death was a near impossible task.

I referred back to an anatomy class I had given him. I explained that life was dependent on the heart beating.

I explained that the man had been foolish and had brought about his own demise due to drinking too much alcohol. I explained that adults partake of drinks that have a consequence on their behavior, and that they lose their self-control.

As I had anticipated Aksel had problems comprehending the concept of drunkenness, he had never encountered anybody in such a state, so was unable to visualize the comportment of somebody under the influence of liquor.

His thoughts concerning mortality seemed to grow stronger in intensity.

"Will you ever die Father?" he asked eagerly, his eyes wide open in wonderment.

I responded as honestly as I could.

"Physically I will, but I am sure to return, I am not like most mortals."

My answer did not appease the child's anxieties. I was the only person in the world he had any connection with. Now I was spreading fears that I would not be around forever, well at least not in my present form.

That night I heard him sobbing in his bedroom. He had never passed a night like this before. The habitual schooling I gave were undertaken in a rather somber mood. He asked his usual questions, but I felt our steadfast bond was not what it was. Maybe I had fallen short of his expectations of me. He'd seen me cure a gull with a broken wing, cure other sick animals caught in death's jaws, he had seen my powers at work.

Another problem increasingly began to intrude into my life. I began to have problems reading from the books I used for his schooling. This impeded on his education. The youth could barely read himself. This inconvenience slowed his progress. I had to change my methodology and began to use books less and less and relied on that chasms of my deep memory. The problem was not just restricted to reading, my vision was getting more and more impaired. I tried to thwart this growing malaise, I was familiar with the use of marigold extract as a natural remedy. Nothing seemed to work, however.

By the time the boy had reached puberty, it was like I had a mist formed around my eyes. Aksel started to spend more time by himself. He would go for long walks, sometimes coming back long after dusk fell. At first I scolded him, but after a time I realized I was powerless to stop him, the boy was growing up fast.

One day he told me he had met somebody while walking around the beach. I questioned him about this person, who was most likely the explanation of his long absences.

It transpired he had met a young girl, a bit younger than himself. They spent a lot of time together at Skagen Cove, a secluded bay.

"Does this young girl have a name?" I demanded.

Aksel became all coy, perhaps regretting that he had opened up a secret.

"Her name is Marna" he told me.

"What of her parentage"?

"She didn't mention her parents." Aksel replied, perhaps getting marked by my questioning.

"Well where does she live" I demanded.

"I don't know father, I just saw her bathing by herself one day and we started talking, as you know I have never met anybody like her before."

"Will you meet her tomorrow?" I inquired.

"Yes, I plan to meet her." He replied, avoiding my probing stare.

The evening was spent in a subdued atmosphere, I suspected the lad's mind was centered on Marna. A new person had entered our lives. He retired to bed early.

The next morning he was clearly not focused on his studies, he even said contemptuously

"Why do I need to learn all this stuff about philosophy?"

I explained that it was important to develop the mind and that it would serve him in later life. "Open the doors of enlightenment and the journey will take you far." I said earnestly. "I might not grow up to be a man like you father" he said. I was fully conscious that fractures were beginning to appear between us. After we had eaten lunch, the remains of a stew I had cooked, he said he was going for a walk along the beach. He left me sitting at the table in deep contemplation. He had mentioned Skagen Cove and suddenly I had this sudden urge to follow him there. I kept a cautious distance as I carefully walked not wishing to injure myself, finally settling on the top of a cliff that overlooked the cove.

I saw him sitting on a rock, all by himself, maybe this Marna was a girl he had conjured up in his imagination, during the course of long lonely walks. This thought pleased me. Then through my blurred vision appeared a girl. To my utter shock she was totally naked. She had long blond hair that cascaded down her back. Her body was svelte and like my son she was tall. I was amazed how clear my vision of her was. No words seemed to be exchanged between her and my son. Suddenly she started to dance. Her movements looked remarkably familiar to me, indeed her appearance was like someone I knew all too well. I was totally mesmerized not only by her beauty but this supple dance that she was performing.

When the dance had come to its conclusion, she walked deftly towards my son. She leant over him and began disrobing the limited clothing he was wearing. She began kissing him before straddling him. I watched her buttocks go up and down rhythmically. Their love session did not last too long, my son was unfledged in the art of love making. They continued kissing and cuddling, but not a word was spoken between them. She dismounted him and beckoned him to join her swimming in the sea. I watched them frolicking in the sea. I decided to take my leave. I couldn't confront my son, after all I had encroached on an intimate moment, but this girl certainly disturbed me.

My son returned late that evening. We exchanged few words. He made an excuse that he was tired and went to bed early. I spent a restless night mulling over the scene I had watched from my vantage point. The pattern of my son leaving and coming back in the early evening seemed to last the whole summer. Once I spotted the two of them closer to our home. Who was this young girl? Was it Astrid, preferring to share her love with our youthful son? I began to develop feeling of jealousy, towards my son. At first I dismissed this feeling as being absurd, but this reflex began to take over me.

I was yearning for the girl myself but realized she would be disinclined towards an aging man whose health and eyesight was diminishing. Such thoughts seemed so unwholesome and there was also the obvious danger my relationship with my son would be fractured further if I tried to make any strong contact with the young girl, who I felt sure was Astrid's reincarnation. I also felt duty bound to warn my son away from this young girl, as it was a relationship bound to hit the rocks, it was a union far too incestuous to my liking.
Time past and my relationship with my son felt vacuous. We were cordial and polite, his lessons were nowhere near the level they once were, however I still deemed them passable.
One evening when we were at table eating poached cod with mustard sauce and trimmings, he suddenly said to me.
"Father, I have something important to tell you, I am leaving you."
I put my knife and fork down, causing a significant clanking sound and felt my body trembling. The boy had recently had his sixteenth birthday, was not ready to join the world at large, what was more I was far from ready to let him go.
"Aksel, what are you talking about, you can only leave on my instructions, your education is incomplete, besides how will you survive, you are still but a boy."

"I am almost a man Father, as well you know, and I plan to set up home with Marna, she is familiar with city life."
Aksel sounded not like a boy, but a man.
"I forbid it" I growled.
Aksel remained resolute.
"There is nothing you can do to stop me" he responded.
I knew the boy was afraid of me. It had taken him courage to deliver his news.
I pointed a finger at him.
"You don't know what you are getting involved with, you will be back soon begging to let you back through this door."
Whatever I said to deter the boy, fell on death ears.
Later that evening I heard him packing his few possessions into a bag.
He left the next day as the sun was rising.
I was alone, solitary, a man left brooding in his thoughts, while craving for a lost son.
He never did come back. I did receive a letter, which I was unable to read, perhaps it wasn't even from him. My days were taken up with chores around the house. Each night I would look out across the bay, wondering if my son would return. The bay always looked as empty as my heart. I was forced to confront myself, my return had not panned out as I imagined it would. Soon behavior even to my rational mind became more fanciful.

Every morning I would conduct lessons to empty chair, the chair where Aksel once listened attentively. I would imagine his responses or questioning, his voice as I remembered it, in my head. If this seemed like ludicrous behavior worse was to come.

My thoughts turned to Marna. I began to imagine that she was besotted with me, in the same way Astrid had been. I imagined us frolicking on the beach. I started walking around the beach naked. I tricked my mind to believe I was with this young girl and that we were in love. A man with a long grey beard dancing about a beach naked, talking out loud to himself, what would any onlooker think? My son's disappearance had sent me over the edge, I was staring headlong into insanity.

Part 6
The testimony of Doctor Asmund Fingus.

As his doctor, for me Amos Toft has to be the most interesting case I have ever come across. A man living by the sea, isolated while fueled with a wild rampant imagination. He was discovered by some monks, walking naked along the beach. When they addressed him, he began to utter strange proclamations. When they returned to the city, they thought it best that they speak to the authorities about this man who they deemed had lost his mind and who they believed was a danger to himself.

Amos Toft was taken by force and brought to me at my hospital.

It was decided that his house should be searched. His wife was found buried in the garden, perhaps her death had brought about his delirious behavior. I was privy to his diaries, which not only made fascinating reading but a real insight into his complex personality. I also conducted many interviews with the man.

The first thing that intrigued me was the fact that he insisted he was the "Master". Looking through his diaries, I noted that one had been written by *the Master.* It was true the handwriting was different. To many it might appear that Amos Toft had been possessed, his mind taken over by this "Master" who had managed to expel Amos Toft from his mind.

There was this constant reference to a son, but further investigation proved that Amos Toft had no son, his wife Inga was known to be barren. However, Amos insisted he had a son, a son who had deserted him. This seemed to bring him deep sorrow.

When Amos Toft first arrived, he was a thin and emaciated man, prone to having long dialogues with himself. He did not fit in with the other inmates. He found it hard to adapt to the institution, he pleaded to be taken back to his rightful abode.

Word soon got out that he purported to be "The Master". I'd had witness many delusional types, those who believed that they were Jesus Christ or God himself, but I had never come across somebody, who seemed out of a bygone age, who was so insistent and almost convincing. His knowledge was inspiring. He told me he cured people, even bringing people back from the dead. Normally inwardly I would laugh at such wild claims, but Amos obviously was no crank, there was often substance to his thinking, sometimes I felt in awe of him. I was supposed to be the doctor, but this patient's knowledge and intellect was overwhelming. I took precise notes of everything he said and read them back over and over again, as they made absorbing reading. It was like he had stepped out of a bygone age. He would have been a perfect case study for historians and those interested by ancient deities, of which he had a vast knowledge.

He quickly became a fixture of the institution. The institution was full of patients beyond help, some would spend the day and night wailing or shouting, prattling away to themselves. The wardens began to acquaint themselves with the "Master". Some began to gently mock him. Hans Fisker would go into his cell saying "Master, Master I have a terrible migraine."

At first *"the Master"* didn't take kindly to such frivolity, he would give Hans one of his glacial stares. However, as time passed he loosened up. A vague smile would reach his lips, and on occasions he might be prone a gentle chuckle. Sometimes he even joined in the banter, retorting "Hans Fisker" the only reason you have a migraine, is because of the inane nonsense emanating from your mouth."

It was hard to unravel this man complex mind, to separate the truth from the fiction. He had obviously had a difficult youth, his fathering perishing to the sea, he talked often about an Uncle Kurt, and an equally colorful Aunt Magda, who had left a lasting impression on him.
I, also, wanted to draw light on what had happened to his wife. He claimed that *Amos Toft*

had murdered her, stabbing her, while she was in labor.

I gently contradicted him.

"But we had her body exhumed and there was no evidence to show she died a violent death"

"But they took her away," said Amos Toft, in the persona of the Master.

"That's not true Amos, nobody took her away, you buried her yourself in the garden, am I not right, and you grieved for her, you are still grieving, this is the fact of the matter, no?"

"The woman was a vessel to carry the child, her body having been appropriated."

"You don't believe this do you Amos, your mind is playing tricks on you, you don't want to acknowledge her death, now do you?"

"If you say so doctor, but the truth is different, and only I know the real truth."

"Your mind seems to be telling you Amos, that the spirit of a man you identify as being "the Master" has entered your body and now controls you."

"Yes, Amos Toft ceases to exist, he resided in my house, the house I was destined to return to."

He seemed to me to be unwavering in his resolve to declare that he was the Master.

"If you are this so called Master, how do your powers manifest themselves, can you make the lame walk, the blind see, the mute speak?"

He laughed gently, "I would never indulge in some unsavory display of my powers, Doctor."

"What of your own heath, you have told some of colleagues that your eyesight is deteriorating, but I find no evidence to support this."
"It is true Amos Toft's body is falling into ill health."
He began to grow wary of my questioning. If truth be told I would often find myself teasing and provoking him, catching him off his guard. Was I really interested in curing him? The man fascinated me so much, I was constantly trying to discover more of him, while less interested in him improving his mental state.

As time passed I got the impression I would not be having many more sessions with Amos Toft, his health as he was aware himself was declining. I struggled to understand him sometimes, he seemed to be constantly fighting for breath.

I was due a short vacation, I was going to see a cousin, who had just given birth. I hoped beyond hope that on return Amos would still be alive and that I could continue delving into his complex personality. On my return, I received the news I had been dreading, that he had passed away, the circumstances of his death had been like the man himself; curious to the extreme.
It was Hans Fisker who recounted how events unfolded.

Part Seven
The Parting

The night was drawing in, when all of a sudden there was the sound of a carriage approaching. At this hour it was an unusual occurrence. Both Sven Sheidler and I watched as the carriage raced down the driveway at speed. The coachmen dismounted and opened the doors, as a man and a woman stepped out. The two walked briskly to the entrance and banged on the door.

Sven shuffled warily to the door and demanded who the two strangers were and the purpose of their visit. They didn't reveal their names but demanded to see Amos Toft immediately. When Sheidler stated that there allocated times to visit patients, the man reacted with indignation.

"Don't be a fool man, let us in immediately."
Sheidler looked at me, fearing some impending danger, despite the hefty metal door that was a sizable barrier between us and the visitors.
Suddenly the heavily locked door sprang open, of its own accord and in marched the two intruders.
Sheilder and I were both incapacitated, overwhelmed with shock.
It was the young man who spoke first.

"This is a sizable institution, take me to Amos Toft immediately."
The young man's eyes bored into those of Sheidler, who bowed to the young man's command, his free will having been snatched away from him.
"This way" he said as if in a deep trance.
We all marched purposefully to the cell where Amos Toft resided.
Sheidler opened the cell.
The young man and the woman brushed past him walked into the meagre cell where Amos had resided over a number of years.
"Father" the young man said, his voice laced with emotion.
The two embraced, clutching one another in an unyielding clench.
I was able to watch this through the gloomy light. At this point Sheidler and myself were irrelevant, it was all about the Father and seemingly a long lost son returning. I heard Amos Toft, gently blubbing, but these were tears of joy at being reunited. The son then introduced the young woman into the conversation. It appeared the young woman was with child. The young woman did not say much, she was of secondary importance. It was clear that as the two men were conversing Amos Toft's health was ailing. He spoke in a breathless voice, often struggling to get words out.

The young man would often say,
"save yourself". The young man demanded
water and a towel. I offered to awaken the doctor,
who lived in the grounds of the institution. The
young man said this wouldn't be necessary.
Finally, I heard the young man simply say, "he's
dead!"
I heard myself saying out loud "the Master is
dead."
To which the young man replied, contradicting
me in a chilling voice, that seemed to resound in
my head he was never the Master, I am!"

Part Eight
" The aftermath"

Suddenly all the lights in the institution went off, and the whole institution plunged into total darkness. Some of the patients began wailing and screaming. The noise was excruciating, I was almost forced to cover my ears, to block out the noise. I had never experienced them so agitated. Sheidler and I felt our way in the dark and managed to light some candles, as we did all the lights went back on, for no apparent reason.

We went back to Amos Toft's cell. Amos Toft was strewn on the floor, lifeless. But what of the young couple? With the sudden darkness they seemed to have disappeared. Sheidler and I mustered up some more men to search for them, fearful that the young man had some devastating powers. A search of the entire institution proved useless. We would have encountered them in the darkness if they had tried to pass us, their footsteps reverberating on the stone floor.

There was no sign of the carriage they had arrived in, equally we checked for any tracks left by the heavy wheels on the soft turf on road, but there were none, despite the constant drizzle that evening. It was like they had never come, both were figments of Sheidler and my imagination. But how could two people imagine the same thing?

Part Nine
Doctor Asmund Fingus' afterthoughts.

Hans Fisker's account of the passing of Amos Toft left me floundering. The mythical son, did he really exist and return just in time for his father's passing? Both Fisker and Sheidler were both loyal employees, unquestionably men of fine repute. Both men possessed limited imaginations, neither being the type of men who would make up wild stories. I found them both highly disturbed by the events that passed that night. These were hardened men who during the course of their careers had witnessed some horrendous sights at the institution, it would take a lot to derange their minds.

Both men started drinking heavily. It wasn't long before they were forced to leave their jobs. I don't know where Sheidler went, nor how his life proceeded. Such a loyal employee to the institution, now reduced to a gibbering alcoholic wreck.

Later I would encounter Hans Fisker, in the center of the city, face down in the dirt, barely conscious. I was later told he had no fixed abode and had lost his mind. I felt obliged to help the man, but it was hopeless. I found him a place to stay, a religious order offered a bed for night, but it was no good, Fisker was a restless

man and was soon on his way, his next encounter
surely would be with death.

Part Ten
Another unexpected turn of events

I was contacted by a colleague in another wing of the institution. He explained that there was a young inmate he thought I would be interested to meet. He didn't go into much detail, it appeared he wanted he wanted me to discover something for myself.

I walked with mounting intrigue to the other wing and made contact with Dr Lund. Dr Lund, a learned colleague filled me in with some details. The patient concerned was a recent arrival. So far he had refused to communicate with anybody. He ate barely enough to sustain himself. It was as if he was in some deep fixed trance, in a different dimension. Why Lund wished me to meet the young man I was mystified.
Shand, the warder walked with us and opened the door to the cell, stood aside and let us in.

There sitting with his back to us, looking out of the window, sat the young man. His long black hair swept down his back, he was dressed in his nightclothes, despite the fact that the sun was bursting through the window, and most of the other inmates were long since dressed.

He didn't speak to me as such, he just managed to penetrate directly into my mind. "I am the Master, the real Master" I heard over and over again. It was at this point that I started questioning my own sanity.

THE NEW MESSIAH

The man appeared to have both a special aura of serenity and yet a commanding presence. He was wearing a spotless radiant white suit and an equally blindingly crisp white shirt, without so much as a crease. As he appeared by the entrance, a sudden shaft of sun sunlight, burst through, clearing a golden path, as he majestically stepped forward on the recently polished floorboards, now drenched in sun-rays, towards the receptionist, who was mesmerised, totally spellbound from the first moment she set eyes on him. A momentary tension existed between them, as she waited for him to break a pertinent silence.

"I need a single room please" he said finally with faltering English, flicking back his long mane of jet black hair, his piercing eyes with the lustre of glistening olives looked into hers. With such eyes, she imagined he could penetrate to the very core of her soul. Checking in new guests, her principal function as a receptionist was a mundane process she had done many times, beyond the point of monotony, but this seemed like a defining moment in her up to now mostly pedestrian life, which had lacked colour, spirituality and meaning.

"How many nights will you be staying sir," she said with a distinct quaver in her voice. "Oh just the one," he replied, in a heavy accented voice.

A wave of disappointment ran through her, his stay was to be short, far too short. "I see" she said masking her disappointment.

"What about dinner, will you be dining tonight," she ventured;

"Some bread and water in my room, would be kind."

"That can be arranged" she said, still totally in awe of him, barely able to look him in the eye.

He was gripping a black leather bag, but did not seem to be carrying any substantial luggage. She hadn't even seen his car draw up. She had been lazily leafing through a magazine, that had salacious gossip, glossy photos of celebrities but limited in content. Her shift was nearly over, it had dragged on, but now she was galled by the fact that she could not attend to this man, just to be in close proximity would have filled her with joy. She would have liked to have been able to make some excuses and just hang around the motel, but she had to visit her sick mother who had resided for the past few weeks in a hospital, with a worsening condition. She would definitely be back for the morning shift, there was still the possibility of seeing him again.

"We need an address and telephone number," she said shakily, as she reached for a clip board, which had a mandatory form all guests were required to complete. Her eyes had followed the way he ponderously signed and provided all the necessary information. As she reached out to take the clip board back, her hand had faintly touched the sleeve of his white jacket. She hadn't planned this, it just happened. It had been the faintest of contacts, but an overwhelming indescribable sensation shimmered and spread through her. It took a few moments for her to recompose herself. "You are not from these parts" she said through slanted eyes, feeling foolish and inadequate at her clumsy efforts to make small talk,
 "what do you do?"

"I guess I am a kind of teacher," he replied in a contemplative voice. That would figure, she thought to herself. He added "I travel a lot, I would like a peaceful room, if possible, one where I won't be disturbed, if you understand."
 "I quite understand," she said punctiliously.
 "I'll show you to a nice quiet room," she said even though all the rooms were neither quiet or particularly comfortable and were certainly of shabby décor, She led him to the one she reckoned would be the quietest, one that didn't

have too much of the constant drone of highway traffic. He surveyed the room, in silence. The room was basic and spartan, a miasma in truth, the carpet worn, with loose threads and parts that had been amateurishly patched up. On the bedside table, next to a lamp emitting gloomy yellow light, there lay a bible, which had a constant thick film of dust on its cover, the edges of the pages stained by coffee and yellow from nicotine. There was a rank peppery smell, she was sure he would have noted, it was almost intoxicating, it could sting the nostrils. Shelley had seen all sorts stay in this room, from travelling salesmen to illicit lovers, often the periphery society, it wasn't a place decent folk would choose, yet here was this man, gracing them with his immeasurable presence

"This will do fine," he said with a faint smile.

"Very well," replied Shelley, "I'll leave you be, have a nice night sir." Shelley took one last fleeting glance at him, just to feast her eyes, and then turned and closed the door, before making her way back to the reception, her mind rapt in thought and wonderment and a kind of rush of euphoria.

Once her shift was over, she made her way to the depressing hospital where her mother was. Every visit to her mother was a heart-wrenching ordeal, tearing her apart. Her mother was the only person in the world she really cherished, and now she just lay in this hospital bed, attached to equipment that monitored her heart, in need of constant surveillance and high dosages of medication, as she was almost certainly on the fresh hold of death. She hadn't spoken in a long time, ever since her stroke. There the occasional signs of recognition, or at least in Shelley's mind but in truth she was in a hopeless comatose state.

"Hello Mom" said Shelley as cheerfully as she could, as she entered the room. Mom's facial expressions didn't move, there was nothing in her eyes to show she was faintly aware Shelley had joined her. Shelley pulled over a chair and sat close to her mother. She had much to say to her mother, to tell her of the man who had come to the motel, but the only way to do this was to have a conversation in her own head, using her imagination, her mother's responses were based on how she imagined her mother would respond and act. It was somewhat excruciating, but it was all she had to alleviate the pain of not being to communicate with her mother. She squatted forward and buried her head in the palms of her hands, she could not look at her mother or the reality of mother's condition would kill the process. It was often hard to keep up the pretence, she often got the feeling, without even looking, that her mother was drifting further away, occasionally she might let out a deep sigh. There was often a cacophony of sounds emanating from other patients, coughing or garbled sounds of old people talking to themselves, perhaps churning up past memories.

The conversation in Shelley's head went something like this.

Shelley "Mom, the most incredible thing happened today at the motel, I think the Messiah has returned and came to stay the night."

Mom "What Shelley dear" (a slight edge of excitement in her voice, a puzzled look on her face)

Shelley "Mom, I promise, he is staying at High Valley, I checked him in."

Mom (a voice with shaded of doubt and intrigue) "The Messiah, how can you tell."

Shelley "I just could, I felt it, he had this presence, he was the most serene of men, he was able to touch my heart, oh Mom he was the most incredible man."

Mom (with a sweet voice) "But Shelley honey, you haven't been to church in years, and now you say you have met the Messiah, the lord sure works in mysterious ways." (She would let out a gentle chuckle).

Shelley "I know Mom, I know, but this man was different, he had an aura, I felt it as he walked through the door, there was this golden light that surrounded him, it was just so incredible Mom."

Mom (in a warbled voice) "My darling Shelley and the son of God, returning to save us."

Shelley "Oh Mom, if you could only have seen him, you would have felt such a warm feeling."
Mom (Mom's voice drops, her features tighten, all the frivolity has now left her)   "Shelley dear, I am not going to be around for much longer, my time is nearly over."
Shelley "But Mom, I need you still, don't leave, stay some time."
Mom "But God is calling me Shelley dear, and I yearn to see your father, you are strong and you have a loving husband and a sweet daughter."
Shelley "Please no Mom, I beg you too stay."

Shelley came out of her almost trance like state, her face bathed in tears. Her mother's face was impassive, nothing had changed since Shelley had entered the room, her expression was frozen. The discourse Shelley had in her head had only managed to make her even more miserable, stirring up her emotions. She kissed her mother on the cheek, her tears deposited on the old woman's face. She rushed out the room and brushed past everybody, even though there were those who showed genuine concern for her sorrowful state. If only she could talk it all through with somebody, the man in the motel for example, wouldn't he above anybody provide some kind salvation? She did not possess the courage to test this theory, after all he had asked for peace and quiet. All she had was to go home to evening with a husband she didn't love and a daughter she feeling more and more estranged from.

She opened the door to their modest house. She could hear them, little Candy always mimicked her father, they would laugh in chorus, in exact sequence, at some dumbed down comedy programme, for a decidedly juvenile mind. It was really like having two children in the house, Arnie was mentally just a child, with an underdeveloped simple mind. He was pleasant enough, some of Shelley's female friends had done far worse in their choice of husbands. Lorna's husband would get aggressive, taking his fist to Lorna, when in fit of anger. Anna Marie's husband was constantly getting her pregnant, a line of six children and one on the way, a house bursting with screaming infants. Shelley had only loved one man in her life. The problem was he was her cousin Neville, it was all too close in proximity and besides Mom mistrusted Neville, she called him "that maverick, that renegade".
She said a man like him would probably spend a vast proportion of his life in a state penitentiary. There were others who said he would do remarkable things in his future, he could be whatever he liked, a leading politician, scientist, or professor or successful businessman Neville had a destiny. There was nobody to compare him to in Valley High.

Compounded to this mistrust of Neville she also wasn't speaking to her brother, Neville's father, their relationship irredeemably fractured, for reasons Shelley could never figure out. Mom could be elusive when she wanted to be, verging on clandestine. Mom had never managed to poison Shelley's mind, but she presented her with a choice, namely Arnie. He was markedly different to Neville and Mom tried to push, dependable but un-flamboyant Arnie into Shelley's arms. The ploy had worked, Shelley had married Arnie, though reluctantly and with deep misgivings.

She had married Arnie simply to appease Mom, she had resigned herself to a prosaic existence. Thankfully Neville had moved to a faroff state, but his memory lingered, it was almost indelible in her mind. She kept his photo in her purse, a reminder of what could have been.

Little Candy was becoming more and more like her father. This was little surprise. Arnie was more out of work than in, finding it hard to hold down a job. While others were buying washing machines and vacuum cleaners, they could barely afford a television.
So it rested on Arnie's shoulders to bring up little Candy. There were two units in the household, Arnie and little Candy and then Shelley, almost an outsider, marginalised and taken for granted.

"Hi honey" "hi mom" they both said in tandem, with the same vacuous monotone voices they employed every time she returned. It might as well be a taped message, triggered by her arrival, it had the feeling of somebody making a travel announcement, it pained Shelley to hear them. Hardly a muscle on their faces moved, their minds and eyes were trained on the frivolous TV show. Shelley mumbled a "hello" and dutifully asked how their days had gone and then left them to chortle at the dumb TV show.

She set about doing some menial tasks, while her mind was elsewhere, partly back at the motel, partly in the drab hospital room with the where her mother was. She had decided long before she set foot in her house she would not tell either Arnie or little Candy, about her day, because they would surely taint the beauty of her thoughts concerning the man in the motel, equally they wouldn't understand the sorrow that was weighing heavily on her mind as to her mother's desperate condition.

This was not to say Arnie was a cold heartless man, he was just so pragmatic. He would go to church almost regularly, taking little Candy with him, but he wasn't a spiritual man, or man who looked in depth concerning any profound matters. Wars, suffering, and starvation never ranked very highly in his thought process, they just concerned other people, in far off lands. He listened to the words the preacher said and he would dutifully repeat the words verbatim, as he was supposed to, in the same way he would laugh went prompted, while watching some comedy programme. Arnie just had these habits Shelley simply couldn't ignore, often he meant well, but always managed to goof things up. After thirteen years of marriage, life was not getting better, it was on a constant downward slope. She had cooked them some supper, read little Candy a short story, that had left little Candy purring for more, had a short banal conversation with Arnie, had left him marvelling goggle-eyed, absolutely transfixed by a science-fiction programme, had made her way to bed and read. Sleep was to elude her. Her mind was too occupied, churning around different thoughts. Warm thoughts of the man in the motel mixed with memories of her mother. She tried to conjure up another conversation with her mother, again in her head. It was hopeless, Arnie kept tossing and turning or letting out loud laboured sighs. Even in sleep he seemed like he was some kind of hindrance

She had got up early. She had paid extra attention to her appearance. The bus ride to the motel had been slow. There was a lot of unusual police activity. The reason for this became apparent when she saw many police surrounding a body concealed by a white sheet. She had only had a quick glance at the scene and had averted her eyes. The other people on the bus started to speculate as to what had happened. She finally arrived at the motel and put on her chequered motel uniform. There were some guests checking out, a cheerful couple with raucous laughs, perhaps holiday makers, they had heavy hiking boots, the air of being carefree. She had questioned Marta who was on night duty if she had heard anything of the man in room seven. Marta looked blankly at her, "no it's been a quiet night, same old, same old." Shelley decided before she officially began her shift, to wander up to where the man was staying. She was somewhat surprised to see his door slightly ajar. She couldn't hear a sound.

She felt miserable about her previous pitiful attempts to engage him some kind of conversation, she wanted to make light of a new chance, she resented her own aphasia. She wanted to talk to him about Mom. There had been a gentleness in his voice, an understanding in his voice and surely if he was indeed who thought he was, he had the powers to heal, even resurrect. She knocked gently on the door. There was no sound. She knocked increasingly louder, but again there was still no response. "Sir, excuse me sir" she called with a voice laced with desperation and concern. Still no answer, just a dense laden static silence.

Cautiously she pushed the door further ajar. The bed had been slept in, the food he had been brought to him, barely touched.

There were some flies dancing and weaving amongst themselves, hovering above the residue of left food. He wasn't there. His bag had gone. She pulled open the curtains to let in some light and opened the window further to gain some fresh air. Perhaps he had stepped out for a walk, but that seemed most unlikely, there was nowhere to walk in these bleak parts, nothing to see. When she examined carefully his bedding, she had an almighty shock. On the white sheets and pillow there was this image, a body in a crucifixion position, evidently the body of the man she had booked in. It was easy to make out, his features were quite clearly printed and definable. "Oh my God" she yelped. Her heart started beating rapidly, her face paled, she sank to her knees. On more careful examination, there were specks of blood where his face was, as well as a rose shaped stain of blood on his chest. There were also marks of blood on his hands and feet.

She carefully gathered the bed clothing. She did not know what to say, she certainly wouldn't tell Marta, who she knew would almost certainly blab, as was her way on discovery of any significant happening in the languid motel. She decided to keep it all to herself, as if he had never arrived at the motel. It was only her who had seen him and motel records could always be changed to suit, easily altered, without any fuss. She put new sheets on the bed and carefully placed his bedding in a plastic bag in a the holdall she always took to work. The morning passed slowly and uneventfully. Her mind just revolved around him. Of course, he never came back. What had happened to him? Had he left her sign? Why the traces of blood? Why the miraculous impression of him on the bed clothes?

The telephone rang. It was Arnie. Her heart leapt, maybe something had happened to Mom. No it wasn't anything to do with Mom. There was an unusual excitement in Arnie's voice, like he was bursting to divulge some important news. He never normally watched news bulletins, but his attention had been drawn to some local news concerning a shocking murder on the local freeway and this obviously had fired his imagination, causing him to take the unusual step of calling Shelley, at work. "Hey Shelley honey, some guy got murdered, can't be far from the motel, just caught it on the news," he blurted out, like a child might at some wondrous discovery. It took a moment for this to sink in, but the activity she had witnessed on the way to work, re-entered her mind, causing her to seek some kind of conformation.

Norman Krabbitz was Shelley's boss. His wandering hands had twice found themselves cupping Shelley's buttocks. He had once tried to manoeuvre his hand up her skirt, but a combination of swift movements and thinking

and screams of "I am married woman" had
repelled him. He had a reputation for going
beyond flirtatiousness. Shelley could be wily
like her mother, using her sweetness and
femininity when the moment required. Shelley
had knocked on his door timidly, with the
helpless look a lost stranger might offer.

"Mr Krabbitz, um Norman, I'm not
feeling so good, I've caught a nasty bug."
Krabbitz was absorbed with some paperwork, an
unattended cigarette smouldered in an ash tray.
He afforded Shelley a quick derisory glance, but
his eyes swiftly returned his papers. She sidled
closer up to him, in an effort to get his attention

"I was wondering if I might go to room
nine and lie down for a moment, just to regain
my strength? I am sure somebody could cover
me, it's very quiet this morning. Her sweet smile
seemed to do the trick." Krabbitz melted, if a
woman smiled at him in such a way.

"I am sure this will pass," she said
pouting her lips, "I just need a few moments."
 He was a crabby, disagreeable man, but he had
his weaknesses and Shelley could often get
around him. He even let her spend more time
with her mother, as a way of winning her favour.
 "Oh well go on Shelley," his voice dropped to a
threatening whisper, " but I might ask some
favours off you one of these days." She thought
she had Krabbitz under control, but he still
always managed to nark her, with his lecherous

behaviour. She scuttled off to room nine, one of the few rooms with a television. She put it on just barely loud enough so she could hear it. There would be a local news bulletin shortly. Sharp dramatic stabs of music heralded the start of the news. It was almost immediate, the man's face appeared. Of course, in her heart of hearts she had expected it, but this did not lessen the shock. She listened attentively to the news reader, her eyes welling up with tears.

"This morning early, there was a shocking unusual ritual gang murder, by the freeway close the small community of High Valley. The victim thought to be Raul Ramirez, a twenty-seven year old Mexican immigrant was found this morning with shot gun wounds to all his hands and legs, as well as a stabbing wound to his chest. On his head, there was barbed wire, as if shaped like a crown. He was left to bleed to death, by the roadside. Ramirez who at one time served a custodial sentence for selling narcotics as well as other more petty crimes, is said to have irked the gangs and the criminal fraternity, with his preaching against violence and drugs, as he denounced his past life and criminal activities, while promoting Christian values. Tributes to Ramirez, a remarkable man, are starting to flood in and flowers are being placed where he was discovered. The Police are mounting a major investigation, but at the present time have not

*released any information as to the perpetrators
of this terrible crime.*

Shelley had heard enough, tears were now streaming down her face. She tried to recompose herself. She returned to Krabbitz's office. He could tell she had been crying, in fact there were signs that it made him feel uncomfortable.
"Mr Krabbitz," said Shelley with a quiet thin desperate voice, "I am sorry but I just have go to home, I am really not feeling so good."
"I see," said Krabbitz with disbelieving eyes, "well I suppose you had better go home, he cocked an admonitory eye at her, I'll expect you tomorrow though."
"Thank you Mr Krabbitz," said Shelley humbly, this is very good of you."
She closed the door behind her and rushed without explanation to the other girls to get the bus. The bus was sluggish, there was still police activity, as well the local media milling about. The place where the murder took place, was not as yet a shrine, but some of the locals had placed some flowers. Shelley kept her holdall which contained the "bed clothes" close to her feet. When she got home, both little Candy and Arnie were as usual absorbed in some trashy TV programme and neither questioned why she was home early. Almost as she opened the door, the telephone started ringing. It was the hospital, there had been slight improvement in her mother's condition, they said not to expect

anything too remarkable, but suggested she should come and visit her mother. She rushed upstairs and put her bag by the bed and changed her clothes. Her mind was working overtime, she was rushing. She breathlessly told Arnie she had to go out, without explaining what had happened. Arnie just nodded, but only showed faint signs of interest.

For the first time in a long time she saw a flicker of recognition as she entered her mother's room. Her mother even tried to speak but no decipherable words came out. She went to her mother's bed and gently held her hand.

"Oh Mom, I am so happy, you have made some progress, I have been so concerned about you." Her mother could not reply, however she gripped her hand a negligible tighter degree and this meant so much to Shelley. She tried to fill in some of the gaps, the things her mother had missed, occasionally her mother might gently nod her head or futilely try to communicate.

She left the hospital, with something she had not felt in a long time, "hope". She had already decided to make a visit to the local church. Her purpose was two-fold, she wanted to prey for the young Mexican, as well as speak Father Brian O'Mally about some of the wondrous things that had happened. She had arrived at the time when Father Brian was hearing confessions. It was perfect, she could

talk to him in the privacy of the confessional, where many secrets were divulged and confidentiality was absolute. Tara O'Grady, a spinster seemed to be taking a long time, which was somewhat surprising, as Shelley could never imagine her committing a single sin, as she was just this faultless little old lady. Perhaps her motivation was to listen to the soothing tones of Father Brian, rather than having her sins cleansed. Finally, she was finished she sheepishly wandered out and began to pray. Shelley had managed to pray for the young Mexican, as well as contemplating about who he really was. Perhaps he wasn't who Shelley had imagined, but some unexplainable things, miraculous things had happened, things she had to talk through with Father Brian.
Maybe he wasn't the new messiah, but he was a kind of messiah and he was at least her messiah. There were the bed clothes for a start, coupled with the improvement, even though perhaps marginal of mother's condition. Father Brian was shrouded in darkness, behind the grill and a linen curtain. Shelley immediately heard his deep heavy laboured breathing,

"Father, it's me, it's Shelley."

"Shelley," said Father Brian, incredulously, "I don't believe we have seen you since Candy's first communion, I had you marked down as a disbeliever." He chuckled at his own jest.

"Not exactly Father, I have some things, I must tell you."

Father Brian craned his head upwards.

"Sins, Shelley, you have some sins to tell me about."

"No Father," contradicted Shelley, "I have to tell you about the Mexican who was murdered."

Father Brian drew in a sharp breath.

"Oh Him, most sad, a terrible waste of a young life." Said Father Brian, with a voice showing scant concern, like he was talking about some triviality, a matter of little bearing.

"You don't understand Father, " said Shelley surprised at Father Brown's flagrant indifference. There was a whiff of stale alcohol, trapped in the confines of the confessional. Father Brian had been drinking heavily the night before, or even during the morning. He had become obviously lonely and felt isolated, languishing in the parish of Valley High.

"What don't I understand" ? said Father Brian, with a mild annoyance in his voice. "He was special, I met him, he was perhaps not the Messiah," said Shelley contemplatively, "but he was like one."
"Now you are being absurd Shelley, said Father Brian rubbing his bald head, your head seems to be full of fanciful notions." Father Brian emitted a sigh, the sigh of a person who is being aggravated by some tiresome irritation. Though

his voice had this soft soothing tone almost
hypnotic, his turgid words could sting and be
hurtful.
"From what I have heard he was just a man, who
mercifully has recently seen the ways of the
Lord, but he is a man with a tainted past, a
common criminal, an immigrant, not a role
model for young people to follow."
Shelley was unimpressed, in fact she was riled,
she hadn't realised Father Brian, was such a
cynic and so patronising.
"There's more Father she said hoping to win him
over, since I met him Mom has made a small but
notable recovery, she recognised me for the first
time in weeks."
"Glad to hear that Shelley," said Father Brian
with mock enthusiasm, "but I can't see any
connection."
"I touched his jacket," said Shelley, "I felt
something, unexplainable, maybe this man felt
my sorrow and had the powers to heal."
"I doubt it somehow," scoffed Father Brian, "it's
more likely your good mother's faith in the Lord,
that brought about this change."
        Shelley was starting to regret sharing
her experiences with Father Brian, it was like
trying to express her emotions to Arnie,
everything was always thrown back in her face.
She continued however, her voice cracking up,
under the strain of trying to feel some kind of
empathy.

"Father, I found something in the dead man's room, his image was somehow transferred onto the bed clothes, like that shroud in Turin, surely you will consider looking into this, I promise you I'm telling the truth."
"The church looks carefully into any kind of miraculous happenings Shelley, there are codes and procedures to be followed, and if you can produce the article, I will make sure the right authorities investigate if there is any credence and authenticity to the object."
"You'll see Father," said Shelley defiantly.
"Maybe I will," said Father Brian snorting sceptically.
 He began to lecture Shelley.
 "I feel you have been through a lot of late, what with your dear mother's state, it's times like these that we need the Lord, as we are so vulnerable, there are too many false dawns and false messiahs, Shelley, believe in the one true Lord and you will find the path to happiness."
Shelley had left the confessional, even before he had completed his sentence. She wanted to get the bedclothes verified, but they wouldn't pass through doubting Father Brian's hands, she would find a more open priest, who would afford her some respect.
 She had said a quick final prayer and had gone home, feeling disgruntled. When she opened her front door she heard an incongruous sound, chugging, vibrating, some kind of machine.

Arnie's face was beaming, his eyes were bright
and his wide yawning grin revealed some lumpy
teeth.
"What on earth is that noise," demanded Shelley
frostily.
"Can't you tell honey, I wanted to surprise you,"
said Arnie enthused, I got it second hand, picked
it up while you were out, it works a treat."
"Arnie," screamed Shelley, her eyes fierce, "what
is it."
"A washing machine of course," rejoiced Arnie
his gawky grin widening even further, "you have
always told me you wanted one and I chanced on
this one going cheap in the local paper, I have
just put in the first load." Arnie looked ever so
pleased with himself, he was bursting with pride,
exchanging scintillating smiles with little Candy.
Shelley fears were mounting, as to what had
happened in her absence. The pattern fitted, it
was typical blundering Arnie.
"What have you put in this new washing machine
Arnie ? Asked Shelley urgently, pronouncing
each word, like a person might to a foreigner,
slowly and clearly. A gigantic question mark
hung in the air.
"Some of Candy's clothes and the bedclothes you
left in our room."
Shelley's face dropped, all the colour in it
drained out, as if she had no blood in her veins
anymore. "Oh my God, please no" yelled

Shelley. Arnie looked at Candy mystified and
both shrugged and frowned simultaneously.

Shelley marched purposefully upstairs. Arnie
remained downstairs, still utterly confused by her
behaviour. Shelley slammed the bedroom door,
her eyes taking in the empty holdall, a gaping
void where the bedclothes had once rested.
Arnie could hear her wailing, intermittently
crying "no, no, no" weeping like he had never
heard before, with the vivacity of a wounded
animal. He thought about comforting her, but he
was unsure if she would welcome him, he had
done something wrong, but he couldn't figure out
what.
"What's the problem honey," he called up.
Arnold replied with in his typical dippy manner
"I only washed a dirty sheet, it was filthy and it
had blood stains on it, surely I did well, I was
only trying to help."

ELSA GRUN

Elsa Grun had done a wicked thing. A very
wicked thing. The temptation had proved too
much. It lay there dormant, in its pink pram.
She'd even imagined it waking up and reaching
out for her to pick it up. She'd even given it a
name, Rita, lovely Rita, her mind resonated with
this name. Before she could rationalize, she'd
picked it up and charged out of the supermarket.

Rita had barely registered the fact that someone other than her mother had whisked her away.

It wasn't that Elsa was a bad person, she didn't have a criminal mind, it was just that her life had not panned out how she'd imagined it would. During her childhood, she'd had visions of the life that awaited her, a husband, perhaps two or three children. She hadn't counted on the mountainous task of finding a reliable man, or indeed the equally formidable task of attracting a man. It wasn't as if she was unattractive, but a quick glance at her, led most men to surmise she was undeniably plain, added to this she didn't have the necessary attributes to be charming or coquettish, so most men passed her by, despite her futile attempts to show her availability.

By the time she'd reached thirty-five she'd joined endless dating agencies and was using the social media to build up possibilities of finding a man. It was not like she hadn't had the odd dalliance. But most men had proved in one way or another, utter frauds.

Hans Tischler, on a short business trip from Hamburg, had expectantly slipped her a note, when she bent over to offer him a beverage, at her job. On the note, was his hotel and room number. He was not an attractive man, with sallow looks, which accompanied his albino-like hair and moustache. His accent was so strong; it was often hard to make out what he was saying.

He also had a tendency to laugh at almost nothing, and try to prove the fact that Germans do after all have some sense of humour. Despite a long list of negatives, Elsa still decided to visit his hotel. When he opened his door, he was wearing a white hotel bath robe and had an inane grin on his face. Elsa almost tried to turn away, but felt committed to follow through. There was the smell of cigarettes, and it was obvious he'd drunk a bottle of wine, to stifle his boredom.

"The flighty secretary arrives" he said extending his grin into a wide smile. Of course, Elsa was far from being a flighty, but she accepted his comment, as a compliment. She let him do all the talking, as she was feeling slightly in awe of him. It was not long however before the telephone calls began. The first call seemed to be in reference to his oldest son Helmut, who seemed to have got into university. The news seemed to delight Hans, who downed a glass of wine in celebration. The next call concerned his daughter Hedwig, who seemed the black sheep of the family, and who Frau Tishler suspected had arrived home reeking of alcohol, Hans said he would have to talk to the young girl on his return, his face however did not show much concern.

The next call was about little Ludwiga, who's tooth had fallen out. Following this call was another family update, on Wilhelmina, who'd cut all her beautiful blond locks off and now looked decidedly like a boy, only days before she was going to take her first communion. Elsa soon lost count of the number of children Hans had procreated, Walburga, Mitzi, Wolfgang, Dagobert, Volkard and Wenzel had all been in incidents of one kind or another. Hans seemed to groan every time the phone rang, surely his wife would soon relent from bothering him soon and he could get down to the real business at hand that of taking advantage of Elsa. After a call concerning Mitzi being unable to sleep and Volkard refusing to say his prayers, claiming he was now an atheist (aged eight), driving his mother into despair, Hans switched off his phone. "I told her zi batteries are almost dead and that I'd forgotten zi charger" he proclaimed with a gentle snigger.

He didn't waste time, he unceremoniously stripped Elsa and used her in the way he'd anticipated, the moment she had stepped over the threshold of his rather dingy hotel room. For Elsa, the sex was somewhat disappointing and she had been dispatched, a short time after the Teutonic one had fulfilled himself, once satisfied he didn't want her to hang around. Of course, she had every right to be bitter. The man was as married and children-laden as any man could be and had made no effort to disguise this fact. While she was getting dressed he reinforced the fact that this was a one night stand, "it was fun vozn't it?" he rejoiced emphasizing "it" double stamping that it was a singular, one off event, not to be repeated. She hadn't answered. Indeed very few words of any substance had been exchanged, since her arrival at the seedy hotel, apart from all the interruptions from his wife. He may as well have raped her, for all the affection he'd shown her, and there was also the striking matter, that no form of contraception had been used. So unless Herr Tishler had had the snip, after all the siblings he'd procured, there was a possibility that another could be on the way, as the man seemed positively spawning children. Though the thought of a possible Tishler offspring didn't exactly appeal to her, at the same time it didn't repulse, as she was more than a bit desperate to have a child. Like most of her relationships with men, this one proved again to be a dead end and Tischler like so many before him an utter fraud.

Her virginity had been lost to a man by the name of Fox. She only knew him by the name Fox, which could have been his family name or perhaps a nickname. He had not only taken her virginity but also the last remnants of her self-esteem, that was even at a fairly young age negligible due to her traumatic schooling, where she was mercilessly teased. Was Fox going to lead her away from her wretched existence? Their relationship lasted one meagre night, before Fox disappeared never to be seen again, however a record of their night of passion did appear in a sleazy film, as the worm of a man had recorded it and had passed it on to a director to use for his next film. Elsa could not understand why people were pointing at her in the street, laughing and mocking her, calling out her screen name "Devine Obsession". In those days, she was strikingly tall and skinny, but it wasn't long before her depression lead her to a routine of comfort eating. She began to bulk up. Men came more and more hard to come by and those she did have were short lived affairs, as with Fox, all were chancers, on the lookout for a quick lay.

There was Sly Gladbotz (aka Count Ernstien Von Schteck) so he told Elsa, the serial bigamist and fraudster, pseudo aristocrat) a man who proudly told her he was a multimillionaire, booked the pair of them into an exclusive hotel, and sneaked out before Elsa was fully awakened, in the same manner as Fox, leaving her to pick up the bill in full total.

She'd met Karl Lutz at a speed dating convention, after some smooth talk on his part; he'd whisked her into the men's toilet for a quick going over, before speeding off, never to make contact again.

Ignatius De Groot, had even talked of marriage, following a short lived holiday romance. Unfortunately, similar offers, were made on an almost nightly basis to almost any reasonable looking impressionable tourist, who caught his eye, in the De Bierwinckel bar, where he worked. He never followed through, the following evening he would be doing the same routine on another prey, and would pretend he'd never met the person who he'd ceaselessly wooed the previous evening. De Groot was frivolous and whimsical and in all likelihoods he was a closet homosexual, who just liked to lark about.

A multitude of thoughts raced through Elsa's mind. Had she been caught on camera, maybe the police were onto her, she would be labelled terrible names, child snatchers get tarred with the same brush as serious criminals, perverts and the like. There was this, as well as where was going to go? She could go to her poky one bedroom apartment, but it would only be a matter of time before the police located her and the game would be up. She had nothing to feed the baby, no milk, no nourishment of any kind. She had no clothes for her. No cot, no toys, not even a cuddly toy. She'd read books in the eventuality she might one day have a baby of her own, but she felt rather helpless now she had a child in her possession things were very different. She was in half a mind to deposit the infant in a police station, saying she'd discovered abandoned in a street, from being cast villain, such an act would make her appear a good citizen. However, thoughts of turning the situation around were suddenly dispelled, when the baby suddenly seemed animated, looked at her and appeared to beam a smile, while looking at her eyes. Elsa translated this, as a sign. She felt the infant had accepted her. Elsa who was walking at pace, managed to smile back. In Elsa's mind, the two had connected, yes they had bonded. There was no going back. Biologically she was somebody else's child, but spiritually she was hers. The child made a noise, "mmm muumma" that endorsed it. "Yes sweetheart" said Elsa, "Mummy's here".

She was in the vicinity of the train station. Jump on a train and she and this new bundle of love she'd emancipated from doubtlessly negligent parents could be the other end of the country, and could start a life anew. She had money saved up in her account. She had no real ties; in fact, nobody apart from her boss would really notice her absence. Once the hullabaloo about a missing baby had died down, she could return, gather her things and she would be free to live the kind of existence, she imagined parenting offered. She arrived panting at the station and looked at times of departing trains. A train to Providence Bay was leaving in fifteen minutes. The station was teeming with soldiers, but they were not searching for a missing baby; far from it, they were patrolling the station, in view of a potential terrorist attack. Religious fundamentalist extremists were trying to create a separatist state, in the south east of the country and were targeting the infrastructure, including significant railway terminals. Being the festive season the soldiers were in a gregarious mood, some even smiled and pulled funny faces at Rita, who was unperturbed by their presence.

She managed to get herself a ticket, buy some basic provisions, like some water and jar of baby food and some diapers. She was thinking like a Mother, she commended herself.

There was no protest from Rita, when the two boarded the train. Other passengers smiled at her, one even commented "what lovely eyes your baby has" Elsa smiled back proudly, as if embraced and acknowledged as a mother. She and Rita were comfortably installed as the train slowly made its way out of the station. Rita stared out of the window, as if mesmerized by the passing scenery. By the time the train had reached the suburbs, she was blissfully asleep in Elsa's arms. She should have been screaming at the top of her lungs, craving for her real mother, but no, she was as settled and happy as any baby could be, unshaken by what had happened. Perhaps her mother had intended Elsa or another with maternal instinct, to chance upon her, to whisk her away, to a better life, the life she deserved.

The ticket inspector arrived, a warm smile on his face, as his eyes latched onto the mother cradling her daughter, beaming with happiness. After he'd afforded a quick glance at Elsa's ticket, he asked "what's she called?" "Rita" replied Elsa, her eyes smothering Rita, as the infant gently exhaled. "Lovely little thing" commented the ticket inspector, smiling broadly, Elsa blushed. It seemed absolute strangers afforded compliments, whenever their eyes set on Rita.

As the train headed north passing factories spewing smoke, there were even abandoned cities, bombed out or simply deserted. Elsa was unfamiliar with where she was going, perhaps she was en route to a depressing industrialized polluted hellhole, perhaps the name Providence Bay, was deceptive.

After the train had passed yet another heavily industrialized grim city, they reached a tunnel. Not long after entering the tunnel, there was a sudden explosion in the carriage next to where Elsa was sitting serenely with Rita in her arms.

All of a sudden, a fireball careered through Elsa's carriage, engulfing it in flames. The passengers in the carriage were soon shrieking in agony, in relentless flames, the carriage diffused with a smell of charred flesh and acrid smoke.

Elsa blacked out but after an indefinite period of time drifted back into consciousness. Strangely enough the train, previously incapacitated, seemed to be moving at speed in the direction of a bright light, the likes of which Elsa had never seen before. This all-consuming light, seemed to also emit a celestial power, as neither Elsa nor Rita, who was now also animated, seemed to be in any pain, indeed they both seemed to be totally at peace. Suddenly the train departed the tunnel and so doing revealed an incredible landscape. There was not the prevailing smog that had prevailed before the tunnel was replaced by a picture perfect radiant blue sky and a bright sunbathed a lush landscape, punctuated by fruit trees, with apples and oranges more the size of footballs. She spotted a large lake which appeared to be filled with milk and honey. Some birds of paradise flew really close up to the train and Rita who was also in awe of these new surroundings smiled broadly. Some zebras uninhibited trotted close to the train, while in the distance there were giraffes gracefully crossing a plain.

It wasn't only the landscape that had gone through a wild transformation, the train itself had marked differences, the window frames were now gold. The seats, which pre-tunnel were a drab grey, were now resonating, a beautiful blue, the likes of which reminded Elsa of the blue commonly seen on peacocks. The entire décor of the train seemed like it had been assembled for royalty.

A man wearing a colorful railway uniform, came into Elsa's vision. At second glance, it became apparent it was somebody Elsa knew, notably Sly Gladbotz.

"Good God Ernstein " said Elsa, surprised to see
the man she knew as Sly.
"Yes" he replied earnestly, "God is good". It was
Sly's voice, but something about him had
dramatically changed, apart from the obvious,
that he was now a railway employee.
"You work on the railways, now Ernstein?"
asked Elsa, still in deep shock.
"In fact," said Sly somewhat sheepishly, "my real
name is Sly, I was a fraud, but now I have seen
the light."
"Oh" replied Elsa, again taken aback by this new
revelation. "Yes" said Sly earnestly, "I used to
run away, now I help deliver people to their final
stop, I will ensure you arrive, you and your
adorable looking baby, there will be somebody to
meet you, when get to the last stop, who will
drive you to your hotel."
"Really," said Elsa, "but I'm not booked into any
hotel."
"Well you are now," said Sly smiling, "it's the
only hotel in town, The Grand Paradiso, run by
the almighty one, need I say more?"
"But it sounds rather exclusive, and it most likely
well over my budget." Elsa said, without anxiety,
but thinking about the practicalities, she was a
new mother after all.
Sly laughed, "it's free Elsa, free ad-finitum,
there's no cost, money means nothing where
you're going."

"Oh I see," said Elsa, confusion written all over her face, while thinking back to the incident when Sly, or at the time Ernstein, had left her in the lurch.

Suddenly music began to emanate from the next carriage, the passengers, seemed to have evolved into a choir, and were accompanied by harps and seraphic flutes. This added to the tranquil atmosphere that pervaded the train throughout.

"You'll no doubt meet some old friends, it's a real catchup place" said Sly cheerfully, adding a few words for the wise, don't look at mirrors, you never know what you might see and apples, the almighty one is a bit particular about people picking apples from the tree of knowledge, it's easy to locate, it's at the back of the hotel, in his private garden, and watch out for snakes, the most deceptive of creatures they can be, you don't want to ire the big man, or you will be banished, thrown out of the hotel and you don't want that Elsa, I can assure you."

"I bought a ticket to Providence Bay" said Elsa, finding it hard to take in, her new circumstances.

"That maybe so," replied Sly, "but you go diverted, an unfortunate incident, but I wouldn't worry yourself, your going to the most perfect of destinations."

"Where exactly?" asked Elsa.

"Well Edenville of course," said Sly.

"Never heard of it," said Elsa.

"You should have done more reading, paid more attention at school, spent your Sunday mornings in Church" said Sly, who Elsa imagined had never set foot in a church and was more likely to be found snooping about sea resorts abounding with gullible rich people.

The scenery remained stunning, more exotic animals roaming freely on a wide swath of land stretching further than the eye could see, a land filled with gold, bdellium and onyx stone, with grapevines, olive trees, and many other fruits. A river, lined by fig trees, pomegranates, followed the direction of the railway track.

"Got to go," said Sly cheerfully, "have some others to help along their journey." Elsa was left holding the baby tight in her arms. Just to think, temptation had got the better of her, and she had stolen, yes that was the only word for it, a baby from a supermarket, perhaps the parents had got briefly distracted, met a long lost friend, believing the supermarket to be a safe place to leave a baby momentarily. But now Elsa appeared to be on a train heading for paradise, a baby resting peacefully in her arms.

The train seemed to be slowing down, it was obvious it was reaching its final destination. The station was punctuated by a vast golden dome. There appeared to be only one platform, implying only arrivals, no departures. The Interior was more reminiscent of a vast cathedral, than a transport terminal. Elsa heard the sound of doors opening and she grabbed her meagre possessions and rather timidly stepped out of the train onto the platform, which appeared to be made from large slabs of yule marble. Some of the other passengers seemed to be carry suitcases with large labels on them, a portly man with "gluttony" in large letters, another who appeared to be young, had "lust" on his, a woman seemed to have a bag overflowing, with "greed" inscribed in large letters. They were all met by people on the platform and as they proceeded to walk, their bags began to disintegrate into dust.

As Elsa, with the baby clutched firmly in her arms made progress down the platform and onwards to an unknown destination a man approached her, closer inspection revealed the man to be Karl Lutz. Despite the fact that their meeting had been all too brief, Elsa was pleased to see a face be-known to her.

"I've come to escort you to your hotel Elsa," said Karl, who was wearing a smart grooms uniform, "my carriage is just outside the terminal."
"Carriage?" queried Elsa. "Well of course," replied Karl, "we could hardly permit any cars polluting a place of such sanctity." Another surprised look flashed across Elsa's face as they walked alongside each other, out of the vast golden terminal.

"There it is" said Karl pointing at a carriage, with six zebras poised to begin the journey. The carriage, gilded in gold, glinting in the powerful sunlight, had a large emblem, "The Grand Paradiso" on it. Karl indicated to Elsa, to sit next to him, the baby looked all around her with great interest. The zebras set off at a fairly slow pace.

"I did a terrible thing to you Elsa, I must confess," said Karl solemnly, "indeed I did a lot of terrible things to many women, got myself excluded from most speed dating events, dating agencies, nobody would take me on, too many complaints from women I abused, but do you know what Elsa, deep inside I felt empty, my soul felt dark and degraded."

"I only fell in love once, in my whole life, Gertha Finklestein, was her name, a former lingerie model with blond hair flowing down her back. What she was doing trying speed dating, I could never fathom why, men seemed to flock around Gertha, and maybe it was some challenge a friend had put her up to. The problem was the allocated two minutes each man had to impress her was far too insufficient.

She was wearing an incredibly short skirt and a tight top and seemed to giggle each time a man made a witty remark. She had one flaw, a scar that meandered down her left thigh, but apart from this, she was perfect. I could hardly wait my turn to attempt to woo her; I was composing my witty repartee, while two minutes dragged on, with a rather plain divorcee, who didn't interest me in the slightest. Try as I might my eyes could not veer away from that scar, how had she come by it? Was it a default she'd had since childhood, surely not, no lingerie model could get away with such a scar.

She shimmied over to my table; hello she said in a soft tantalizing voice, I'm Gertha. I introduced myself, and suddenly blurted out, and your scar, how did you come by that scar? I could not have begun in a worse way, but she seemed only mildly taken aback. She told me she had been on a photo shoot in some North African country for some high fashion magazine and was stood next to a young tiger, whereupon the young wild cat had suddenly turned on her and sunk its claws in her leg. The pain had been excruciating, but there had been one positive, it had ended her superficial career as a model.

With this long story recounted, I had hardly any time to speak of myself. Our time was up; she was moved onto another table, where a rather loud businessman, with perspiration streaming down his face, was sat. I had to endure a few meaningless encounters, before the conclusion of the speed dating event. I was totally surprised that I was given her contact details. Never afraid normally to call women to arrange a date, with Gertha an overwhelming nervousness came over me. There was something about her, that made me feel horribly inadequate or was I for the first time falling in love? We began gingerly dating, but it was a long time before she invited me back to her apartment, in an exclusive residential area. I'd imagined the apartment would be filled with pictures of her, imagining her to somewhat narcissistic, but in fact to the contrary, her apartment was minimal but stylish.

She was brisk and to the point I'm not going to sleep with you Kurt, if that's what you are thinking. I'd never been confronted with such words and all I could manage to say was 'I see'. She still huddled up close to me on her sofa and began to tell me about some of the places she had visited. I found her really captivating; but I was lost as to where our relationship was heading.

Will we at any point be sleeping together? I demanded, rather anticipating the answer to be a firm no. She replied well Karl, will I be another of your two minute romps; what's in it for me…sleeping on a damp patch, waking up to see you have disappeared? My best friend runs the speed dating agency warned me off you, seems you have cultivated quite a reputation, I wanted to see if you would try it on with me.

It seemed my reputation had quashed any chance of me sleeping with Gertha and yet we still met up the next day and the day after. Then finally much to my surprise she invited me into her bedroom. Our lovemaking was wholesome and unlike any previous experience

I'd had with a woman, it was like our two souls were enmeshed. As I left her apartment, we made plans for me to come back that evening; whereupon surely we would surely make love in the same manner. My whole day was spent thinking about her, I could hardly wait to finish work and go over to see her. I decided I would surprise her with a present and drove into a multi-storey car park to acquire a suitable gift. Having acquired a bracelet, I was sure she would be pleased with, I went in search of my car. The car park seemed deserted, however as I approached my car, I suddenly heard some footsteps. As I struggled with my car keys a figure approached me at speed. 'Give me your wallet, your phone, your car keys, and I might let you go', said a voice in a menacing tone. I turned around to see a man with a baseball bat. He jabbed the bat into my stomach winding me. I complied with his wishes, nether the less he began beating me severely about the head. Faggot he called me over and over again, with each blow reigning in on my head. When he felt he'd had enough of this unwarranted beating he shoved me under another car.

I wasn't discovered until much later, my face disfigured and unrecognisable. I required some delicate surgery to reconstruct my face, but most significantly it wasn't just my face that had been damaged it was also my memory, to such an extent I could not say who I was. I had been discovered literally in my clothes, with no other possessions or forms of identification. Nobody came to identify me. I had no strong connections, I'd only just joined the company I was working for, perhaps they just thought I didn't like the job and had just moved on somewhere else. As I began to recover I wondered if any family would come to collect me, perhaps I had a wife, maybe even a few children, looking at my face in the mirror told me I was of the age to be married and a parent. Nobody came for me. Doctors told me my memory might return at any point, quite suddenly.

When I was physically much better I was told it would be better to start my life in the country, some peaceful town or village would be far more appropriate for a victim of violence. A doctor even suggested a quiet town where I could go; a friend of his had a farm and was looking for somebody to help with the horses. I began my new life in the country. Little frissons of memory recall sometimes entered my head. Being helpless and being savagely attacked. Further beyond going to a shop to buy something. Beyond this having strong feelings for somebody. There were sketchy memories of my childhood as well as being a student at college. Everything remained vague and unsubstantial. I settled into my new life. I found my new life agreeable and even learnt how to drive a horse and carriage. Before long I was accomplished with handling horses. My memory faculties were still far from complete, but I was leading a good life, having made some friends and was well attuned to the country by now.

Time passed. One day following a violent head ache, I went to see the local doctor. Sat in the waiting room I started to flick through some magazines. There wasn't much choice in magazines so I glanced at a celebratory gossip magazine. Suddenly my attention was drawn to a well-tanned beautiful woman, looking lovingly at a husband and two very young infants, an angelic boy and a girl. The headline read world famous film director Herb Slimbucker with his gorgeous wife and ex lingerie model Gertha. Somehow I knew this woman meant something to me. I surreptitiously ripped out the page and stuffed it in my pocket. A short while later more of my memories began to fall into place. I remembered why I was in the car park and that I was going to see Gertha on the night of my attack. Why hadn't she come to visit me in hospital?

Further memories revealed Gertha had been one woman in my life amongst many. It seemed obvious, I had not arrived at her place as planned and she had simply given up on me. Essentially I was paying the price for all my previous indiscretions. My life before my accident had been wasted; I'd just played the part of a pseudo-playboy, with no regard for any of my conquests. I was ashamed of my pre-accident life, when memories came flooding back I felt sickened. I began to despise myself. Then one day I arrived here and now I drive people to their final destination.

They passed through a large arch, surrounded by golden walls and proceeded along a long driveway, surrounded by the most beautiful garden Elsa could imagine, with fruit trees, lush greenery, with new born lambs with blindingly white fleeces flittering playfully about, fountains with water shooting up into the air, and were soon at the entrance of the Hotel Paradiso. Like the railway station before there seemed a lot of activity and bustle. The Hotel seemed to seemed to have an inordinate number of floors as if it extended ad finitum. "Impressive" said Karl to Elsa, who was astounded by the façade of this endless hotel bedecked in shimmering gold leaf. "No need to check in," said Karl with a chuckle, "because there's no check out." Pointing at a large notice board, he said "there are a few rules you need to observe and the Almighty one, might want to say a few words to you at some point, the Almighty one always makes a point of welcoming in new intakes ." "So I've heard," said Elsa. "The lift boy, will show you to your room" said Karl, who had another pick up to make. "See you Elsa, it was nice talking to you, getting a few things off my chest, so to speak and once again please forgive me for what I did." "Apology accepted" said Elsa as she walked towards the lift, baby clutched firmly next to her chest.

The lift doors opened and outstepped none other than Fox, in a smart blue uniform, with a hat that had Hotel Paradiso in gold lettering. "Elsa" he said sheepishly, "I'm going to take you up to your room." Of course the hotel had a seemingly uncountable number of floors and Fox tapped in the floor number. "It's not like your normal hotel, Elsa you understand" said Fox as the lift began to descend. "You will also experience a transformation, because of the number of residents, you will shrink to nano size, however you will imagine everything is normal scale, there is nothing to be afraid of, it's just a necessary procedure. Of course, I owe you a big apology, I know I did an unforgivable thing. My life was a littered with diabolical misdeeds. Taking a young girl's virginity then profiting from it, is not something I was proud of, indeed my life was full of shame, now I'm consigned to monotonously going up and down in this lift throughout eternity, as a form of atonement. Some of my discretions came back to haunt me. One day I was quietly watching television when there was a sharp rap on the door.

I opened the door and standing before me was a man, with striking blond hair, bulging biceps and a scowl on his face. Stood next to him was a woman, petite compared to him, both were bronzed. Stood behind them was an adolescent, with spiky peroxide died hair, a sallow face, his clothes worn and seemingly unwashed, he had a malevolent sneer aimed at me. I didn't have the time to ask what they wanted. The muscular man thrust the youth forwards over the threshold of my house with a hefty shove and said "you got my woman pregnant and this is the result, now he's your responsibility, we never want to set eyes on him again." I took a quick glance at the woman but her face was totally unfamiliar try as I might to rustle up a connection. In all probability I had slept with her, but I certainly couldn't recall her face. On the porch lay a scruffy suitcase, I presumed the youth's belongings and sitting on this suitcase lay an envelope. 'Read, scumbag'!   said the man in his booming voice. In the back of a family saloon car sat two angelic looking children, presumably the half siblings of my alleged son. They were smiling and chatting cheerfully amongst one another.

I opened the envelope and pulled out an official looking document, with birth certificate in bold letters. I read, Mother Ena Gratbratz occupation secretary, Father Randell Fox, occupation unknown, address unknown. Son born 7.30 am at Stromf hospital, named Egon Gratbatz. Why they had taken so long to track me down was one debatable point and why they were desperate to be rid of the scrawny youth was another pertinent point. The name Ena Gratbatz also meant nothing to me, but then I never made much effort to remember names, but I could normally place a face.

The muscular man ushered his wife to the car, opened the car door and sped off, leaving me with the adolescent known as Egon. "Well take a seat" I said to the youth, not knowing what to do next. Egon sat down, but didn't say a word. He appeared to have a terrible cold and was constantly sniffing. It seemed to me that he needed a doctor, his health condition was a low ebb. He reached into his pocket and pulled out a battered looking packet of cigarettes and fumbled to find a lighter. I don't really like smoking in my apartment, I said in a firm but composed way. The youth seemed undisturbed by my request not to smoke and muttered under his breath, I smoke, get used to it. Our first confrontational situation had passed with me realising I would have little if any control over him. Egon, isn't it, I said to try to induce some kind of conversation. He afforded me a quick cursory glance before drawing in a large intake of smoke from his lit cigarette. It was obvious that conversation and Egan didn't go together. Do you go to school or perhaps college, I enquired. Used to, he muttered, got kicked out. All this didn't bode well. Do you want to watch television, or perhaps you're hungry I said cheerfully. Hate television and I'm not hungry, he replied. Striking up a conversation proved nigh on impossible. Having smoked one cigarette, he was soon onto a second one. What about I coffee or perhaps a tea I offered, again he declined. I gave up on any forms of hospitality. After a long painful silence, he declared he was going out, in one way for me it was a relief, trying to connect with him was heavy going, in another way I felt fear, what was he going to do? When would he return? We've only just met, is that such a good idea, you don't know your way round these parts I said. I'm going out, now leave me alone, you are starting to get on my nerves, like mother and her stupid husband did, now butt out asshole.

With these delicately put words, he stormed out of my apartment, leaving his suitcase and the smell of his cigarettes. By midnight he still wasn't back. At three o'clock in the morning the doorbell rang and on the doorstep stood Egan with a police officer holding him. This toe rag says he lives here, is that right? Well yes, I replied edgily. Caught him shooting up in a car park, it seems your son is a junky, said the officer, his voice laced with hatred. He carried on, this time I gave him a bit of a kicking and took his smack off him, next time I won't be so lenient, he'll get banged up, call yourself a father do you. And with that the police officer marched away. You take drugs I demanded Egon, the answer was evidently yes, you only had to look

at the youth. What if I do, hissed Egon, it's not your fucking concern. If you live under my roof, I think it is. You've never been bothered with before, so why the fuck now, said Egon venomously. I didn't know you existed I protested. Shouldn't have fucked Mother, Egon said, as if admonishing me. Well I did, or at least your birth certificate says I did, so now we have to try to get on with things, as best we can. You do what you like, replied Egon with a sneer, I knew I'd hate you even before I met you.
I guess you hate everybody, I said looking at his torn t shirt which had a hand written slogan *This world is toxic, I hate everybody.* I guess so, he replied caustically adding but you in particular. Why me I asked innocently, cos you fucked off, didn't ya, he replied searching for a cigarette packet. He cursed when he could only find a broken cigarette. After exchanging a few more venomous slurs, I brought up the subject of his drug habit. "Have you done heroine before I asked. "Nah" he replied, it seemed like an opportunity, and I am a bit bored of hash, speed and coke. He made it sound like he was making some kind of graduation. Have you been doing drugs a long time I enquired, since I was about twelve he replied, with pride in his voice. How do you pay for your drugs I asked curiously. It's obvious ain't it, I go on the rob, nick things, Mother's jewellery, go through people's pockets,

that kinda thing. It was obvious I'd spawned a callous monster.

Putting these concerns to one side, I ushered Egon upstairs and showed him the spare room, where he would sleep. I didn't sleep much that night, turning around in head was what to do concerning my alleged reprobate son. It was the weekend and he didn't rise until midday. I said to him good morning he said nothing, he just scowled. Do you want some breakfast, I asked, Nah he replied, don't eat breakfast. A coffee perhaps, I offered. Nah, don't drink coffee, could do with a cigarette. I don't smoke I said, never have. He shrugged. Do you have plans for today, I asked innocently. Nah nothing special, what do you care, he said spitefully. Just asking, I said, thinking whatever I said would met in the same manner. I thought it best not to engage with him and I went about my usual routine, while he seemed to stare into space, as if in some kind of trance. He left without saying a word and I profited by hiding any valuables I thought he might get his hands on to maintain his drug habit. Our time together passed in a similar pattern. If he was warming to me in any way, I couldn't detect even the most modest of changes.

One evening while I was watching some inane television programme, while he was chain smoking while sending me hateful looks, while appearing to be disinterested by the TV, there was a sudden roar of motorbike engines.

Fucking cool, Hells Angels Egon said as the motorbikes skidded to a halt. Much to my surprise, indeed horror, the riders all clad in black leather marched to my front door, at the front a man carrying an axe. There was a rap on the door. Gingerly I opened the door, while fearing for my life. We've come to make a delivery said the man with the axe, a delivery I parroted, paralysed with trepidation. Your daughter, said the man with the axe. It seems you got Zelda here up the duff, she's fed with the responsibility of bringing up Raz here, so she's passing on the responsibility to you, dig it. Apart from taking on a band of Hell's angels, my choices were limited. Raz proved to be a fifteen year old girl, very advanced for her age. She was wearing a short skirt and noticeably had very long legs, that seemed really tanned. However worse was to come, she came with two accessories a vicious looking dog called Gash and a cat called Shag. The reason for the dog's name was to become evident fairly swiftly, when the brute sunk its teeth into my ankle. The cat's name's pertinence was also soon to come the fore. The young girl immediately made her distaste for me evident from the outset. Why do I have to live with this asshole she complained, jabbing a finger at me. Your Mother does not want you anymore, so you're stuck with your father, dig it girl.

The man with the axe was not one to waste time and soon the gang were revving up their engines and were on their way. Egon seemed to find my new situation amusing, delighting in my new despair. Another uncouth teenager set to upset my life even further. Raz, I never got to know her real name nor could I place her mother, proved to be horribly obnoxious. In a way Egon's disapproving eyes and disenchanted manner were far less irritating compared to Raz, the bitch from Hell. Egon this is your half-sister Raz, Raz this is your half-brother Egon, I said hardly believing the words coming out of my mouth. The teenagers stared each other, but said nothing. Would you guys like some food. Not fucking hungry they answered in tandem. Wouldn't mind a beer, if your offering piped up Raz. Aren't you a bit young to drink, I retorted. Fuck off replied Raz, been drinking beer since I was eight, I could drink you under the table, no trouble. So now I had a drug addict son and an alcoholic daughter as well as two mangy animals, could life get any worse?

Needless to say I inherited the job of looking after the cat and the dog. Raz and Egon barely acknowledged each other, or so I thought. After a while I started to notice things missing from my house, notably bottles of alcohol, but also some valuables, including some I'd inherited from my late father. I confronted the two teenagers, both shrugged and said 'not my problem, nothing to do with me'. Threats to severely punish the culprits fell on death ears and were met with mocking laughter. If things carried on like this I would be slowly but surely stripped of my possessions, fleeced by these two shady juveniles. Arriving back home from work late, the living room and kitchen were noticeably devoid of the errant teenagers. Maybe they were out, but no, I heard panting noises from above. I walked purposefully upstairs. To my horror through the crack of the spare room door I saw Egon on top of Raz, both naked.

What the hell do you think you are doing I shouted at them, watching them going at it like rabbits. What the hell do you think we are doing, replied Raz, fucking of course, something you should know about, but apparently you fucked off as soon as the fucking was over. How dare you I shouted at her, feeling more enraged than I had ever felt in my entire life, despite the fact that what she said rang true. Egon stopped pumping away, let out a perfunctory groan and reached for his cigarettes and lit one up. This is none of your business anyway said Raz sitting up on the bed, running her fingers through her hair., flaunting her svelte body But he's your half-brother I exclaimed, as if I had newly discovered morality, while thinking of the consequences of Raz getting pregnant under my roof. Maybe said Raz, adding he's not a bad fuck. I left the room feeling utterly disgusted, while at the same time

it appeared I had finally stumbled on parenthood.
The teenagers finally appeared downstairs,
holding hands as if to provoke me further. Should
I bring up the subject of contraception I
wondered. You did use some kind of protection
Raz, I hope. Yes Egon used one of those rubber
things, replied Raz. I'm glad I muttered. The
following day, I was invited by a neighbour for a
barbecue. It was a relief to get away from the
amorous adolescence. However when I got back
I was due for another shock.

One of the adolescence had parted
the nest, taking with him anything he could find
of value, as well as my car. Raz said calmly,
Egon's fucked off, couldn't hack it around here
much longer, doubt you'll see him ever again you
should be happy. Surely you must be a bit upset,
I said to her. Not really, she replied, he was quite
a good shag, but I've had a lot better. Was she
always trying to antagonize me, or was she as
depraved as she made out? Time proved the
latter, a stream of men, some the same age as me
and adolescents began to arrive on a regular basis
and I was powerless to stop this flow, though
technically she was under age and the law was
being broken. There was Olaf Spitz, who owned
a tattoo parlour, who I suspected fell in love with
Raz. He gave her a free tattoo on her left bicep,
'Fuck off and die' inscribed in unmissable bold
letters. Soon he was dumped and Gerd Fink an ex
rock star, a total spent force who employed his

time recounting stories of tours he'd made, the groupies he'd had, sometimes three at a time, mixing fiction and truth. He told Raz he'd introduce her to a big time agent, she'd need singing lessons but she had the charisma to be a star. The idea soon fizzled out like the romance, Gerd got back together with the queen of all groupies Sheena Feltz three times Raz's age, a grandmother and Gerd and Raz were history.

Of course, Raz bunked off school systematically, but what could I do. The school was also at a loss how to deal with her. They suggested psychologists, some parent, children counselling, sterner parenting, tough love. I was at fault, too liberal, but parenting was something that had been imposed on me. I was quite simply way out of my depth, unable to stamp any authority. Whenever Raz made the effort to be at her supposed home we had furious arguments, screaming matches that the whole neighbourhood were party to. Once she even got violent, picked up a kitchen knife, I had to restrain her. What could I do? Call the police. She was getting wilder and wilder, more out of control.

I found my principles enlarging through my alleged offspring's lack of principles. Raz also stole like her half-brother and even managed to make use of my credit card, how she got hold of my number I'll never know, but one day I caught her rifling through my letters and

private affairs. The girl was sly and resourceful, I
had to give her that.

One day like her older half-brother
she fled the nest. I asked about, nobody knew
anything as to her whereabouts. Perhaps she had
joined Egon, or left in search of her Mother and
the Hells angels. It was part relief part sorrow for
me. She did leave something to remember her by,
I was the permanent custodian of two scraggy
animals, Gash and Shag.

I realised I had failed at parenting, but
more significantly I had also failed in life. My
life had been an unmitigated mess. Perhaps there
were other Egons and Razes littered about,
perhaps they too would appear from nowhere.
My past haunted me.

After an immeasurable period of time,
the lift slowed down its speedy decent. Elsa felt
different and put it down to change in scale Fox
had mentioned, the surroundings remained to
scale however. Elsa, said Fox remorsefully, I am
so sorry for what I did and I guess I talked too
much about the problems I went through, I am
sure you would never have gone through the
same with your little angel there. Fox gently
stroked the baby's head and she smiled sweetly
back at him. I best show you to your room, then
Elsa. Elsa followed along the long corridor which
had a burgundy coloured carpet and as with the
rest of the hotel was lavishly decorated.

Eventually they arrived at a room with Elsa Grun in large gold lettering on a name plate. Fox opened the door, there was no lock, why would there be, there wouldn't be any crime of any description. The room was no unlike anything Elsa had seen let alone stayed in. It had a sweet smell, as it was full of exotic flowers giving off a strong scent. The room looked out onto a large garden with a large tree, the one that Sly had talked about. It was the most impressive tree Elsa had ever seen. There was everything Elsa could ever need. Elsa noticed something, maybe a picture or a mirror, that was covered with a purple drape. "I wouldn't touch that if I was you" cautioned Fox. "Well I'll leave you be and let you settle in and once again I'm so sorry for what I did" he left head bowed and headed for the lift. There was a cot placed next to a large bed and finely decorated flasks full of milk and honey. Elsa bathed the baby in a tub, the first time she'd ever bathed an infant. The baby seemed to relish the bath and seemed totally content in her new environment. Elsa dried her off and laid her in the cot, before gently rocking her to sleep. Once assured the baby was asleep, Elsa helped herself to some fruit. The succulent fruit tasted delicious. There were some instructions next to the bed indicating meal times, in the grand dining hall, which served each floor. Elsa of course would remain with the baby. It wasn't long before she also fell asleep.

Her dreams were vivid and full of beautiful landscapes filled with exotic animals, the likes of which she'd seen on the train journey. Her grandmother featured in her dream but looked more youthful than Elsa recalled, indeed she was exuding great beauty.

The baby slept through the night and both she and Elsa woke up to bright sunlight which gilded the garden. Elsa picked her up from the cot and held her tightly in her arms. Then she fed her with milk and honey and some fruits, all of which she seemed to relish. Having played with her for quite a while Elsa put her back in her cot for another sleep. While the baby peacefully slept, Elsa had a bath. The bath was not a typical bath, it was the shape of a shell and had constantly running water, at the perfect temperature. Elsa luxuriated in the bath. Having dried herself and dressed herself, there was a gentle rap on the door. She opened the door and stood in front of her was a man dressed in an orange uniform, with *Humble Cleaners* in bold letters. "My God" exclaimed Elsa, as her eyes took in the sight of Hans Tischler, laden with cleaning apparatus. "Yes it's me" said Hans Tichler, you must be a bit surprised to find me working as a cleaner, it's a chastening existence, but one I merit, none the less, as the life I led was dictated by money and business, I was a proud man, but my pride was also my folly. Where did all my money really get me? Almost all my children ended up despising me. I was always away and when I was home, I had no time for my children and I treated wife terribly, as you fully know. My soul was black and iniquitous when I entered here, but with my new work, I feel cleaner and emancipated.

Frau Tischler hasn't arrived yet. She's even with another man, Herr Shling, the postman. The man was delivering letters of condolence, when my wife had a fit of sorrow, right in front of him. The runt of a man used her vulnerability as a pretext to gain her affections. He took her in his arms and held her tightly. After a while her emotions changed from melancholy to amorousness. I had provided her with many children, but at the same time I had blatantly neglected her and when the first opportunity arrived for some intimacy, she took it with grasping arms. 'How do you know this' questioned Elsa, full of wonder. Hans pointed at the burgundy drape, you just need to pull at that drape and all will be revealed, but for me, it was a mortifying experience.

"What a complete mess I made of my life" rued Hans, look at my children, Ludwiga for example, what an angel she was as a child, I'd half expected her to grow up to be a nun, at the age of twelve she wanted to be a ballet dancer, she got a place in a top school, what did she end up doing, she became a pole dancer, but in a sleazy strip joint, sleazy men slipping her money, a shady existence, a life gone wrong. Wilhelmina joined some cult and we never got to see her again. She disowned her family and was brainwashed beyond hope, another life gone wrong. Walburga simply gave up on life, became a hermit in the wild, told me she was ashamed of her capitalist father, before she went she gave up all her worldly possessions. Mitzi, my fertile earth mother daughter, got pregnant easily and by the age of seventeen she already had three children by different men. God knows how many children she has these days, even offered to be a surrogate to couples who couldn't have children. Wolfgang became a habitual criminal, mostly fraud and internet crime, eventually the police caught up with him and much to me and wife's shame did time in prison, the story made the newspapers. Dagobert was another of my children who turned against me, we could hardly be installed in the same room, without an argument flaring up, he never told me his sexual orientation, but I had my suspicions. Volkard was always sponging my money, him and his wife Vanya also, he made out it was my duty to furnish him with money, that he'd had a deprived childhood while he hardly did a day's work, in his life, told me he was a struggling artist, I couldn't make any sense of his work for the life of me. Wenzel the mysterious son went to Africa and never came back. Phoned home once a year, short empty meaningless conversations, which would leave my wife crying after she put the phone down. Said matter of factly he was married, there were doubtlessly grandchildren, but we never got photos, we could only imagine what they looked like. Then one day we got a phone call from a woman named Caz, told us he'd died, shot in the head, then set on fire, seemed he'd been an arms dealer. Why go to the funeral, there were no remains and Caz tersely said it would be a small private affair, and never even thought to invite us, the parents.

Having gone through all his children's foibles and failures, Hans sighed. "Well it seems you are now well down the path of motherhood," said Hans, peering at the baby. "Well yes," replied Elsa before asking, "what happens, will she grow and develop like any normal child?" Hans laughed gently, "in this place time is completely different, it moves incredibly slowly, days seem like centuries, she will age, but it seem almost negligible, to you." Elsa's enthusiasm to ask more questions to Hans about her new circumstances. "What about sex, do people have sex here?" It seemed a strange question to ask, especially to Hans, who had blatantly used her and doubtlessly many other women besides. He laughed again. "The sex here, is a bit different, nothing like earthly sex. It is usually done in the garden, some stick to their earthly companions, some choose those who are their spiritual kins. It is performed by way of touch of hands and what follows is wave after wave of love, until both reach an unimaginable crescendo, that last the whole night through, it is like nothing you have ever experienced."

"Who will I get to meet, Hitler, Jesus, Gandhi, my ancestors?" Asked Elsa with marked excitement. Once again Hans laughed. "Hitler," he replied "is not a resident, along with any other war lord, arms dealer, mass murderer and usually the most lauded humans are preoccupied in their new existences and have little interaction with lesser mortals. You can get to know your ancestors, but in some cases it is not always advisable, it's too much to take in, most of my ancestors proved not to be residents."

Hans had finished his menial job of cleaning the room and was bidden to clean another resident's room. He gave Elsa a warm smile and left the room.

Elsa settled in more and more, relishing motherhood as well as the wondrous benefits bestowed by the hotel. She watched those with physical abnormalities, be instantly cured in the spa of the hotel, the lame were able to walk, the blind could see. Each day brought a new joyful discovery. Her life on earth had been drab and often excruciating, her new existence bore no resemblance to what had been.

One day while she was feeding the baby, there was a sharp rap on the door. She stopped feeding the baby and walked to the door and opened it. There stood Ignatius De Groot, but looking nothing like she remembered him. For a start his long blond locks had changed to short black hair, in a very conformist style. His youthful face looked stern and solemn, his eyes locked onto to Elsa, in a way that suggested he had been dispatched with a purpose. His skin was sallow and not tanned in the way it was during their last encounter. He was wearing a prosaic suit, a pristine white short and a black tie, with a tie pin the form of a cross.

He offered a pale smile and said "Elsa" before making a sign of the cross and said "this is not going to be easy." For the first time in a long time, Elsa felt a rush of fear. "Ignatius, what do you want?" asked Elsa. "It's the baby, Elsa, you know you can't keep it, that is, if you want to remain a resident here." Elsa was shocked, she clutched the baby to her ever stronger.

"You know it's not possible, the Almighty one has decreed, you have to give her up, of your own free will, it is that simple, you took something that was not yours." "But surely this Almighty one can see my heart will be broken, it's too much to ask of me," Elsa said in a desperate voice, tears streaming down her cheeks. "The Almighty one has his rules and regulations, he has a world to run and has done so over centuries." "But surely to take away this baby, would be a cruel act, please don't let this happen" pleaded Elsa. "As you well know Elsa, this baby is not yours, let's see what you did when you took this baby." Ignatius walked towards the purple drapes and pulled them apart. There appeared to be a mirror, but slowly images started to come into focus. The setting was the supermarket. A young mother seemed to be racing around desperately shrieking the name of her lost baby. Pain was written all over her face. The staff of the supermarket came to her aid. The young woman was so distraught, nobody could placate her. "You see what you did?" said Ignatius with an accusative voice.

Later the young woman was seen making a telephone call, presumably to the father of the child. Then the police arrived, a gruelling process of interviews. Later on CTV Elsa was seen taking the baby, the quality of the image, must have proved unhelpful to the police. Next, two anxious parents making a national appeal on television for the return of their missing daughter. "Imagine what they were going through" said Ignatius, adding it was a foolish thing to do Elsa."

"I know, replied Elsa, but I simply couldn't control myself, so many years alone, so many unreliable men, all I ever wanted was a baby, surely what I did was not so terrible, just a bit of terrible misjudgement, totally off the cuff, out of character." "Now you can make amends" said Ignatius. "I wish I could, but it will tear me apart" replied Elsa.

Suddenly Ignatius' voice transformed into Fox's voice, "Give the baby back"
Then it transformed into Sly Gladbotz's voice "Give the baby back Elsa!"
Then there was the voice of Hans Tischler booming "do as you are told Elsa, give the baby back"
After which it changed to her father's voice, said in a very patronizing way, "Elsa, darling, Daddy says give the baby back, do as Daddy says."
Finally not from the mouth of Ignatius, but from the mouth of the baby herself, in a soft cherubic voice, "give me back, I need to go back to my real mother."
It seemed like everybody was suddenly against her, Elsa still held tightly onto the hand of the baby.
"Now give her to me and you can become a full time resident here in this hotel, Elsa, you know it make sense" said Ignatius in his own voice. A million other voices seemed to echo Ignatius' words. Slowly Elsa handed over the baby. Suddenly she felt she was going through a new transformation. There were distant voices that were gaining in lucidity. Figures seemed to be bending over her. It was obvious she was no longer in the hotel, and it was apparent she was now in some kind of hospital, there were even some smells to verify this. The hovering figures were in white coats. "She's coming around" she heard one of them say. She wanted to use her will

power to wrestle herself back to her previous state, back to the hotel, but it was hopeless, this new reality was taking further hold on her and there was nothing she could do.

"Elsa Grun" a stern voice said, before repeating "Elsa", "Elsa" "Elsa" each time with progressive fortitude. It didn't take Elsa long to realize it was the voice of a doctor try to bring her back to consciousness. The man then tried to flash a light in one of Elsa's eyes, before repeating the same action in the other. No words came from Elsa's mouth, she was still clinging on to the hope she could remain in the hotel and not in the surrounds of a hospital.

"You're in a serious burns unit, I am afraid you were caught up in a serious terrorist attack, I am afraid you have some extensive injuries." After assimilating this rather devastating piece of news, finally Elsa managed to force some words from her mouth.

"And my baby, what has happened to my baby"?

"Your baby" demanded the doctor quizzically, there was no baby in your carriage, in fact it was mostly filled with rather elderly people and nuns, all travelling to some religious convention, there certainly was no baby found next to you."

DARK ANGELS

It was as if an angel of death had swooped down and had slain all those below, sparing only one. Over 6,826,300,000 people annihilated, by a deadly virus, that had taken less than a month to work its way across the globe, a bacteria transmitted firstly by flies, then birds, then other animals before, culminating in human to human epidemic. There was no time for any kind of animal cull, nor the production of some kind of vaccine, for this disease, as it spread so mercilessly fast. This angel of death had lunged and its hand showing no remorse, causing carnage to all in its path, the rich, the powerful and the mighty, without distinction. The victims would begin with a fever and as death approached they would be in a state of delirium, shouting out inordinate pained sentences, that meant nothing, other to themselves.

The structure that existed within nations previously systematically broke down. No Governments were prepared for such pandemonium, which had arrived in a surge. There was no hiding place, no readily available antidote or provision. While the army and police forces of nations were impotent, cities burnt, forests burnt, normal life simply broke, down before all succumbed to this disease, or food shortages. Factories, power plants, and hospitals were forced to close down, or were looted by lawless mobs. Television channels soon ceased to broadcast, their final words being stark and doom laden, giving the postscript of a world that was dying all around, just the pronouncement of that final epitaph.

There was talk of this contagious virus being developed, the fusion of two lethal viruses. However nobody stood up and took responsibility. The instigator was faceless, invisible, unaccountable. The words "terrorist attack" might have been muttered at the onset, but such words seemed to be inept and futile, in connection to the enormity of what was happening worldwide, without exception.

There were no bonafied explanations, just feeble conjecture. Preachers tried shouting their empty meaningless words, in empty places of worship, as cities bells tolled the chimes of doom. All airplanes that had not crashed were soon grounded, the flight crews were quickly overcome with the virus. There were no safe havens many flights were refused landing privileges in other countries.

Fear and suspicion was spreading as fast as the virus. Your neighbors were unwelcome, even with a desperate plea for help, after all they could contaminate you and your family, a locked door was your only refuge. There was no compassion left in the world, only pathetic hopes of survival.

However with food shortages and this reign of anarchy and people falling all around them, some chose suicide. Others preferred locking themselves away, some helping their children die a painless, more tranquil dignified death, cradling them in their arms, some singing gentle songs, as they took their last breaths and past away.

The world had been tested before, world wars, natural disasters, nuclear disasters. People throughout history had had visions of what the apocalypse might be like, and now it had finally arrived, but it was still an unexpected intrusion, that ultimate horror on a wide unprecedented scale.

Professor Lyle Krueger was in his late fifties. His mother had died giving birth to him. His father had taken this as a sign, that this newborn child was a curse on the world. Though he had loved Lyle's two older brother, like no father could love his sons, from the onset, he rejected Lyle, often just referring not by his name, but with the words "that boy". And how Lyle felt all this rejection in deep down inbuilt antipathy. It was just plain on his father's face, no words were needed to express this. Lyle took comfort from the fact that the nanny his father brought in to look after the children, showed some morsels of affection, but far less than the affection she held for Lyle's father and his two siblings.

Lyle grew up in the role of the outcast. His efforts went unrewarded. His exceptional grades never even warranted a pleasing smile or a word of praise. He was marginalized by his peers, heckled with the words "freak" or "weirdo". His entry into the world had been traumatic and his childhood had followed in the same manner. Nobody could have imagined this constant "rejection", being shunned for no reason by his fellow man.

It was not as if he had unpleasant looks, he had smooth faultless skin and shiny radiating eyes and a smooth sounding voice that had dulcet tones. It was perhaps something deep and embedded that he transmitted to others that led them to eschew him. His brothers academically had been less than average, and yet they were often lavished with undue praise. They would go onto follow prosaic, meaningless jobs. They were not ones to leave their marks on the world, but Lyle Krueger sure was.

His excellent grades took him into a prestigious medical school. He thought this milestone in his life might give him a new credence, but it was just the excuse his family had to cut their ties even further. Letters to his nanny also never got returned. An invitation to his brother's wedding never arrived, and later there was to no excuse for this major oversight. It was like he was living in a far off country to them.

He was the one blemish on the family that nobody could forget. His father had even remarried, the young nanny he had employed. Lyle took this as a sign, he had moved on, but he could never move on, even with the passing of time, and the joy of a new wife, he would forever harbor this pain of his first wife's passing.

It was not only his family, but also women, who cruelly rejected his subtle overtures to them.

Hannah Steiger had everything going for her. She was the daughter of an eminent scientist, who was surely destined to follow her parent's footsteps. Her grades had been exceptional and she had beauty besides. She had slowly been offering crumbs of encouragement to Lyle, flirting with him, despite the intensity that he afforded to his work. He had even piped up enough courage to ask out for a dinner date. She had been cool about the idea, but he finally managed a "yes" out of her. His vision of her, was that of a kind of goddess, but one with an intellect to match his own. She would be the great beacon of joy he'd strived for all his life.

Her late arrival at the dinner table had brought an unwelcome surprise. She was drunk or maybe even intoxicated on some kind of drugs. She had hardly made an overt attempts to excuse her tardiness. She had swanned in and barely looked at him in the face. He had tried to make some conversation, but his only subject was that of the module they were undertaking, "cell structure; mitosis; meiosis, gametes and fertilization, all hardly appropriate to the dinner table."

It was not long before there was an interruption. Hannah shamelessly answered the call and got up, leaving Lyle, lonesome at the table. After five long excruciating minutes, she returned, seemingly animated.

"Ralph's going to hang by," she explained.

"By Ralph, you mean Professor Fisk," he ventured, with a trace of disdain in his voice. Fisk was young, by repute brilliant, his accent to the top echelons of the university had been rapid. Lyle assumed he was taken, as there was talk a fiancé, indeed the Dean's youngest daughter, was said to wearing an engagement ring.

Lyle had meekly protested.

"I thought this was a dinner date."

"A dinner date talking about cell structure; mitosis; meiosis, gametes and fertilization," she mocked.

Ralph Fisk arrived, in the same animated state as Hanna had shown previously. He gave Lyle a dismissive weak smile of recognition. His eyes were all over Hannah. Doubts about Hannah began to circulate in Lyle's mind, was she really what people made her out to be? He had built up this demure image of her, he had imagined he could discuss pertinent scientific subjects, it was what united them, they were akin in these matters or so he thought. He had discovered she was superficial, though demure in the lessons they learnt together, but outside the scholastic walls she was a flagrant flawed character. This made him despise her and Fisk, who was now petting and whispering crude utterances in her ears. Lyle was excluded, he was strictly the third unwanted party, the blip on a frivolous evening, fuelled by lust and drugs and alcohol as the other two let down their hair and indulged in this murky relationship they had going on. As a scientist Lyle was fully developed, but as a man he was grossly immature, he held infantile grudges.

"You're a bit of a dark horse Krueger," said Frisk condescendingly, "whatever did you think you could achieve by asking the lovely Hannah out."

"I thought we had a bond, we have scientific interests in common."

"Let's just cut to the chase Krueger, you wanted to take this pretty young thing home, where upon…"

Hannah cut in and complained while smiling broadly.

"Come on Ralph leave him alone, I am sure his intentions were quite innocent and let's not forget, he is destined for great things."

"Surely," scoffed Ralph, "but this guy is no fun and not pleasant company, I suggest he goes back home and reads up on some scientific dissertation, by some intellectually challenging boffin and leave us be, he's cramping our style." Ralph inched closer to Lyle and spat out, "take a hint wacko and get the hell out of here." Quietly Lyle stood up. He sedately put some notes on the table to pay for the meal, including some wine, he had meticulously chosen, which Hannah had barely touched.

He felt for days, the other students whispering behind his back, mercilessly mocking him for his feeble attempt to woo Hannah. He was just too earnest, too serious, for even a class full of supposed brilliant minds and scientists. At the same time he felt he had learned another form of rejection. He had tried to reach out to somebody, who really could not careless about him and was more enamored by a man who would leave her for another conquest. Though he was the victim, the innocent party, he was besmirched, ridiculed, where as he rightfully deserved adulation for his mind and what he could offer this world.

He was treated with coldness not only by his fellow students, but the professors were wary of him. He could make them look inadequate, with his fine-tuned mind, his sharp analysis and profound understanding of subjects others were trailing behind. He was found immersed in books, delving deeper than any of the other students, even those of the highest echelon. As ever he was the outcast, shunned, lacking respect, despite his grades, that surpassed any students in the colleges long illustrious history. Always this pain was welling up inside him.

His father died, and though his brothers for the sake of propriety invited him to the funeral, he was just the "other brother", "the runt of the litter". He shed some tears, but they were not for his father, they were for him and the intolerable life he'd led. His father had been extremely rich and despite leaving the bulk of his money to the brothers he adored, he begrudgingly left some money to Lyle.

Lyle did not squander this money, he invested it well and soon built up his own business, which flourished. He was able to build laboratories and employ researchers. His name was growing steadily as well as his reputation. He was most of the time totally absorbed in work. He was not an easy person to work for, he was demanding, some said totally ruthless, most could not keep up with his standards.

He had his own private sanctuary. All other employees were barred. People often wondered about him. He was like no other person they had come across in their lives. Many felt uncomfortable in his presence, there was an intangible fear of him. His words were few and sharp and he was getting ever distant and remote.

A glimmer of happiness appeared in his life, after years of toil. The invitation to present some of his ideas to a top American science federation. The subject of his talk was the blueprint to save countless lives, the world over, ending disease. Of course he was not going to delve into exactitudes, but he was going to leave his marker and surely finally reach that goal of his to earn the rightful reverence of his peers.

He took an unnatural step for him of drinking some whisky, as he stayed in a hotel. He was also on some kind medication, prescribed to alleviate his mind that was racked with clinical depression. While ensconced in his hotel room, he heard a familiar voice. It was unnervingly and blatantly brash voice of Fisk. His mood which had once resonated with hope, now sunk. His mind returned to that night, the night Fisk had humiliated him, turned him against women, who he now deemed as being treacherous schemers, never to be trusted. Fisk was laughing, sharing some puerile joke with another delegate.

How he hated Fisk, always had done. How had Fisk been invited. He was far from being eminent, his lectures were usually colorless and rudimentary. Fisk was a net worker, a hustler, who despite lacking substance knew how to work the system. He could share a glass of wine with an attractive woman, but his contributions to science were limited. The sound of this man's voice made him sink another pill and down another glass. His whole mental balance had been sent spinning and there was no way to stabilize it.

He had woken up the next day through a thin unrewarding sleep. His eyes felt heavy. He hadn't bothered with breakfast. He preferred to scan his notes again. He found it hard to focus. Fisk's voice echoed again, down the corridor. Men and women were laughing, as if he held them in the palm of his hand.

Oh Christ no, thought Lyle, *this is so excruciating*. He had taken a shower, hoping it would remedial and refreshing. Drying the globules of water, he felt no better. He'd previously felt sure the other delegates would be sympathetic, all attentive to what he was telling them, but now doubts lingered, Fisk would be among them, spreading poison, destabilizing him. He would be scrutinized, judged with severity. They would all surely try to pit their wits against him. All that wisdom he possessed would account for nothing, especially if Fisk had got to them already. He felt sure that a plot had unhatched, the air seemed thick with complicity. History was full of misunderstood people and "if onlys". If only Adolf Hitler had not been rejected by the Vienna Academy of Art. He felt angry that he of all people had to carry on this lifelong fight for acceptance for basic standing, in a world that he had so much to offer.

He listened to some of the opening speeches. Yes some had some good points, but

were trivial compared what he about reveal, the culmination of so much research. He heard his name being called. His moment had arrived. He stood up, somewhat groggily. His body felt heavy. His head hurt.
There were some people from the press and media, who would be tuning in to what he had to say. Some cameras flashed as he made his way to the podium. He was bedazzled and lights aimed at the podium were also boring into his eyes. His mouth was dry and he had metallic taste in it. When he finally reached the podium, he tried to compose himself. There was a weight of expectancy. He had the reputation of being reclusive, an unknown quantity to many. He had never given interviews to the press, despite the significance of his company and its success.

When faced the audience full on, he had one vision in his head. They all had the same eyes, those disparaging eyes his father had. He was looking at his father's eyes, but multifold. His heart was speeding up. Oh yes Fisk was well placed but equipped like the others with those disapproving bulging eyes. His mouth seemed to be twisted in a snarl. But it wasn't just Fisk, he felt hatred towards, it was everybody. He hated them all, without exemption, those he did not know. It was indiscriminate hatred. Thoughts entered his mind. He had arrived with the intention of doing so much good for the world. However it was an undeserving world. It was a world that had by and large rejected him. What if? What if he was turn the opposite direction to his original idea, of saving millions of pitiful people. To unleash, on the world something devastating, something that might release him from his torment, from all those year of pain. At last his mark would be left on the world. There was no going back, he had crossed a line.

He turned from the audience, without so much a word uttered. He heard his name being called, as he charged out of the conference hall, "Professor Krueger, Professor, are you all right, is there some kind of problem?" He could imagine Fisk, smiling, inwardly laughing, but this was of no consequence, he had plans, plans of great bearing. He had the tools to carry out such a cataclysmic plans. He felt like he had more potency in his body and mind than he had ever felt. At last he would be able process some kind of happiness. He was ready to commit the most hideous crime of all time and his mind was even showing the remotest signs of conscience, just pangs of hatred and desire to cause devastation on an unprecedented scale.

He could not wait to work on this ultimate project. He would spare himself. There seemed little reason to go the way all the others would go. He would create a lethal bacteria, but at the same time he would produce the antidote, to which he would exclusively administer. He was going in a direction nobody had been before, the ultimate statement. There was nothing for people to suspect him, he had the shield of a respectable business. None of his employees would dare to question him. He would close the laboratories down soon anyway, concoct an excuse about safety, amongst the pandemonium that would ensue, this would not present a problem.

He locked himself away, almost working round the clock. The breakthrough he required came quickly, he already had the prerequisite knowledge, he just needed to make the final touches. He needed to test the antidote. The monkeys he used to test it on, showed a tangible resistance, it seemed full proof. All was now set in place. It was summer and a particularly hot one at that.

He administered the lethal bacteria to crates of flies. There was a large market, selling fruit, vegetables and livestock. It was close to an International airport. The food was exported internationally. It was not so far from a river and a huge industrial zone. It seemed the perfect location to release the flies. Unbeknown to him and totally fortuitously industrial action meant the market was in a terrible unattended state. There was rotten matter all over the place and other flies were already present and profiting. To most people this scene would have been abhorrent. There were large clumps of animal dung, scattered about. There were sea gulls scavenging about. It was a calm humid night with no wind. Unfortunately, he was not alone. There were some vagrants and travelers, some bedded for the night. His white van had attracted some attention. As he unloaded a crate full of flies, the vagrant shuffled towards him. This was an unwanted intrusion.

"Get away from me," he shouted at the man, who continued his slow shuffle. There was hatred and venom in his voice.

The man had a bundle in his hands, perhaps some food, which he was holding onto determinately. The man was not sure on his feet and slipped. He seemed incapable of standing up. This gave Lyle the idea, he had earned enough time to release the flies and get away. Nobody could spoil this moment.

He opened the crate, while the vagrant still struggled to get back on his feet, he had obviously consumed a lot of alcohol. Lyle heard him mutter, almost apologetically.

"I wanted a cigarette, that was all."

The flies flew rapidly out of the crate in different directions. Some settled on the vagrant, attracted by the bundle of food he held. He pathetically tried to swat them away. It was almost risible. Lyle almost burst out laughing, he managed to contain his laughter, or he have might of become hysterical. He did not want to jeopardize his endeavors, by attracting unwanted attention, with a show of frivolity. After all, in his van there were still unopened crates of flies. To be dispersed by his next place of call, the port.

If only the absurd vagrant knew he was swatting away angels of certain death. In a way to Lyle, this was a man of significance, as he was surely to be the first carrier, either him or one of the others, They were surely susceptible, disease ridden and defenseless, he had heard violent coughing. The flies were just everywhere, mingling with the other flies. Settling on the dung or the rotten fetid vegetables or other decaying matter. Over the next few days there would be thousands of new flies hatched, and two weeks down the line, a new batch, they are prolific breeders. They would start to spread out. Other animals would be infected. And before the world knew it, they would be faced with an unprecedented epidemic on a massive and uncontrollable scale. Lyle's white van roared away into the night.

As planned he stopped by the port.

There were more people about and he felt wary not attract interest. There was livestock penned in, in readiness to be exported. He chose a dark alleyway, close by to the livestock and released another batch of flies. He moved rapidly back to van. As he was driving back, he heard the gentle buzz of a fly.

This fly managed to annoy him all the way back to his final destination, perhaps it had been trapped before he set off. When he retired to bed he was exhausted but exhilarated. He few days later he would head south and cross the border. There was no problem getting past boarder control, his company frequently delivered medical supplies, he had all the paperwork. The crate of flies were well stashed away, amongst boxes of medication, bound for the capital. He arrived in the suburbs of the largest spread city in the world. It was a humid night. There was few people about, but it was a deprived neighborhood. Some children, with faces of angels with dirty torn clothes were playing in the street, occasionally shrieking, weaving about amongst the rubbish strewn randomly. He unceremoniously opened the crate of flies, unnoticed, as if he was invisible and watched them go their different directions, some settling on the children, they patted them away and carried on their game. He then drove back through the night.

A few days later he headed north. He wanted to spread his lethal virus, right in the hub of government, to see society disintegrate, for countries to fall apart, for death to be everywhere, to settle his account with the world, that had rejected him by and large. Death at the epicenter of power would decapitate those who might find measures to alleviate the ensuing epidemic and its carnage. On his journey back he would release more crates of flies, in the suburbs of sizable cities. When they flew away, he felt a rush of elation.

He was excited when news started to filter through of "unusual deaths". This was later followed by talk of the spread of a "lethal epidemic" which soon got labeled much to his gratification, a "super epidemic".

Bacteria seemed resistant to seemingly all antibiotics. He was not so happy when Fisk, appeared on one of the main news bulletins to give his take on this new virus that was taking its toll at an ever increasing alarming rate. He said they "were not ahead of the bug but in time they would" with his usual flagrant confidence. The world authority was at a loss, clutching at thin straws, pathetically inept, deemed Lyle.

He liked to watch them squirm, baffled by what he had set in motion. For a change he felt so much power running through him, he was the master, the world now dancing to his tune.

Initially it was large cities that succumbed to the virus. However, it soon spread to rural and then remote areas. Countries tried quarantining, banning travel, blocking their borders. There was no turning back the tide. Lyle Krueger had succeeded in doing something nobody had achieved before, mass murder on a global scale. In countries in the African continent and India, the virus swept through rapidly and incisively. Lyle had dismissed his work force and was cocooned in his laboratory, watching everything unfold, until there was no more broadcasts. The electrical power soon went down, but he had made provision for many eventualities. He was well protected and lacked for nothing. He could get on with his research, unbothered. The telephone never rang. He could never be disappointed again, there was nobody who could jolt his perfect existence.

He went for months and months, just locked away in his heavily securitized laboratory. He never saw daylight. There was no need in this inner sanctum. He just lived in his own head. Perhaps the thought of the human-less world that now existed outside. He was not feeling any guilt, there was not one person who he felt any empathy towards. His brothers, well they had just caused him pain accumulated over years. Other scientists, well he had felt like a leper, a pariah with so few invitations to share his work, his papers rejected by science journals, with curt replies.

When he did venture out, it was spring. There would normally be the din of traffic, a cacophony of sounds, of a city alive and bustling. There was nothing, no lights, no power no movement. There was abandoned cars, dead animals lain on the roads, in different states of decay. It seemed obvious to Lyle, his virus had succeeded in the way he had anticipated, clinically. The Human race was now something of the past. He had made his statement. He felt joyful with a bizarre warped sense of pride and satisfaction, his work was now done. He went back to his laboratory and played music, Moonlight Sonata, by Beethoven. If only Beethoven had been the blueprint for human beings, he mused the world would have been so much better, no need to suffer fools and frivolity.

He seemed to sleep well these days, so much baggage had been dispersed, so much weight off his shoulders, so much clarity, whereas before life had been so cluttered and full of human frailty and defaults. He felt more relaxed. He could go for walks and as long as he kept up his antidote, life held no fears. He even had relaxed as to the security. There was nobody who could harm him, no threats, at least not human ones. He slept in total darkness, he prudently used his electrical generator for daytime functions.

He was deep in sleep. He had worked hard the day before. He had carried on his working life, as if nothing had happened. He lacked lab technicians but this was a trifling matter.

Suddenly he thought he heard a voice, say something. Of course this was an absurd notion. He had not heard another human's voice in months and after all he had seen to the demise of the human race. This was surely a voice that had intruded on a dream. Everything was just a

dream, he was not in a conscious state. The voice would go away, it had no right to impinge on his sleep and dreams. He had grown use to this perfect solitude. He heard his name being called. "Lyle Krueger, it's you isn't it?"
He did not respond, he was still in a state of denial and in a dreamlike state. A nagging thought entered his mind. The voice, which reverted the spacious room, was echoing and distant, was one that he was familiar with. It had the hallmarks of Fisk's voice, he was pretty sure of this. This sent a shudder of pain throughout his body. He felt like he was pinned to the bed, as if paralysed. He had the insurance of a pistol under his bed, but he room was pitch dark and would be so until the morning, when he would open the shutters. He felt compelled to answer the voice, but maybe he was just going through the process of a dialogue, embedded in a dream.
"Get out of here, you have no right to be here!"
"I have every right, I am here for the sake of justice."
"Justice," snapped Lyle, "for what?"
"We both know what you did, the virus, mass murder on an unprecedented scale, consigning the world to its ending; you have a lot to answer to?"
"You seemed to have come through unscathed, perhaps I miscalculated."
"That you didn't," retorted the voice, "I just got lucky, I hit upon something others didn't."

"You could have saved millions," said Lyle with
a sharp accusatory tone, "why didn't you?"
"I barely made it through, I was sick,
incapacitated, it was the side effects of the drugs
I administered," replied the voice, adding, "I
don't have too much time left."
"So now you have come back to haunt me have,
to derange me as you have always done," said
Lyle mournfully.
"I've got my revenge," replied the voice.
"That's impossible," responded Lyle, "I am fit, I
well unless you have a gun and shoot me, what
can you do to harm me in this darkness."
"Have you been eating well recently," demanded
the voice coolly, a voice laced with a sarcasm.
"Yes of course I am well stocked for food and
can produce food in the future." Replied Lyle,
unsure where this surreal conversation was
leading.
"While you have been venturing out in the world,
those precise twenty minute walks you take
regularly, I've been busy, I've learnt a lot from
you and now you will die in the same manner of
those you have slaughtered."
"You have been in my laboratory, meddling?"
bellowed Lyle in a fury, nobody had ever
ventured into his sanctuary.
"Yes," replied the voice almost dispassionately,
"and now you yourself have been infected with a
virus, a variation of your own work, lethal

enough to finish you off, poetic justice don't you think?"

"You said you were dying yourself, why kill me off," said Lyle bitterly.

"You more than anyone who has walked this world, deserve to die, in fact you deserve to die a million times over, but I managed to keep alive one of my sons."

"One of your many bastard sons," interjected Lyle venomously.

"A small matter in light of things, he unlike me is of good health," he responded, "well to the medication I gave him, he is surely the only person who will survive, but he is prepared to go on."

"This is insane, you are just in my head, this is a dream, when I wake up you won't be with me," shouted Lyle.

"Believe what you like," said the voice, walking away, leaving Lyle in his bed in a state of agitation.

He took time to go back to sleep and even then it was a restless sleep. All that composure he had built up, all that closure he'd felt had been fractured.

He woke up the next morning feeling not only exhausted but also markedly sick. He could not eat any solid food, he constantly felt like retching. The sickness also brought with it apathy, which meant he almost resigned himself to the inevitable death that would soon ensue.

Perhaps it was just one terrible dream, all those tainted memories of Fisk, surfacing in his consciousness. However the sickness would go away, indeed it seemed to getting stronger hold on him and he did not have the strength to fight it. He was dying but someone out there was still alive. He wasn't the last man to walk this earth, it was someone else.

THE DROWNING

He had been swallowed by the sea. He was a fisherman. It was the only life he had known or wanted but the sea had taken him. His body had never been found. There had been a violent storm. They had watched as he had been taken further from the boat, by the currant, churned about in the sea. Nobody could have survived in such conditions, though he was a strong swimmer, with big powerful arms. The sea could give and the sea can take away. His wife had grieved. It's always the wives who are left behind.
She was young, an exquisite beauty with cerulean eyes that captivated anyone who came into contact with her. They had been teen age lovers. When they were old enough they had married. They had decided to bide their time before having children, but their love for one

another was as strong and unquenchable. They lived for each other.

She had been attending to some sewing. She always paid such attention to his clothes. The slightest tare and she would darn it. She prided herself in the way she cared for his clothes and wellbeing. She had heard the rumble of approaching footsteps. Then there was an urgent pounding on the door. She had placed the needle and thread on the table. Her heart beat rose steadily. Maybe she had sensed the worst before she even opened the door, as all fisherman's wives do when the news they never want to hear is about to unfold.

Three of them had stood in the doorway. They had been silent at first, not wishing to spring the bad tidings they had deliver. Casey had spoken first, his voice little more than a barely recognisable whisper. "He's disappeared" he said "he's been lost in the storm." Spontaneously tears trickled down her face. She would have liked to have appeared brave in front of these men but she could not contain herself. Connor added pathetically, "we are so sorry, there was nothing we could do, the sea was bedevilled tonight Misses."
And then they had left her. She was left with emptiness, the house had no joy any more. He would never return, it was finite. The rain lashed against the window pain, as if somebody was throwing little pebbles. The days that followed

produced no body. She could not even see his face for one last time. To say her last goodbye. God could be cruel and the sea as his instrument of cruelty and heartlessness. She felt resentful. She was a widow at such a tender age, it just wasn't fair. Her future looked so bleak.

As time passed, the house began to become a reminder of her loss, sometimes even sounds in the night, the sudden creek of a floorboard would give her false hopes, maybe he was returning. But he never did.

She made plans. She needed to get away. To find a new place to live, a place which would not remind her of her loss and sorrow. She would go and live her life in the city, a place where she would not be constantly reminded of the sea. Her family were heartbroken at her parting. Her father had driven her to station, in almost silence, he was deep in thought and with a heavy heart. She had watched pathetically as they wave to her as the train drew away, tears tricking down his face, he was not a man who would normally cry.

She had found a room in a house. The proprietor was of Polish origin, with an almost incomprehensible accent. She found him to be slightly lecherous and overbearing. He had shown her to her room and she had unpacked her meagre possessions. She had placed the last photo she had taken of her husband, next to her bed. She was weary after the journey and she would have to preserve her energy to find a job. She slipped into the course sheets of her bed clothes and fell asleep. She still dreamt of her husband, he was still in her dreams and thoughts.

She was woken up in the middle of the night by the sound of loud voices, of giggling. It seemed like there were two woman and a man. "Oh Oliver, you are so naughty." One of them trilled, then giggled uncontrollably. They were all drunk, shamelessly drunk.

Oliver seemed to be relishing the attention he was getting. She heard the sound of him taking out some heavy keys and opening the door to his apartment. It was her first encounter with Oliver. The walls were paper thin and she could hear them whispering giggling, she even heard the sound of their clothes dropping to the floor. There was the rhythmic creek of bed springs, eruptions of pleasure, heavy sighing, more drunken ranting. Then they seemed to drop off into a calm sleep.

She tried to picture Oliver, but she couldn't. He intrigued her. He seemed to have something special about him, she hadn't come across his type before, a city man, a man who was obviously confident with woman. A man with a strong sexual appetite. A man with wit and humour and charm.

Days passed and she still hadn't met Oliver face to face, they kept different time tables. She was out in the day sorting out a job, he was doing whatever he was doing, probably sleeping off his excessive night before.

Finally they crossed on the landing. She wasn't disappointed, his face lived up to the intrigue she had carried over a number of days. He was handsome, like nobody she had never seen before. Where she came from faces were worn and lifeless, bleached by the sea but this man had devilishly good looks. His clothes were smart, without a single trace of a stitch to repair, no worn part.

She also relished the fact that he smelt so good, he was sweetly perfumed. His hair faultlessly slicked back.

He had offered her his hand and had gallantly shaken her hand, "my names Oliver" he said proudly as he peered deeper in her eyes. She was breathless, overwhelmed by him. She had almost been speechless. He hadn't stood on any ceremony, he just simply said

"I know a great little bar near here, as my new neighbour I'd like invite you, to get to know you, how does that sound?"

As a widow, she felt inclined to refuse, for the sake of propriety, but she couldn't.

"Ok" she said meekly.

"See at eight o'clock sharp" he said doing a twirl, and flashing a smile.

She had spent time preparing for the night. She had bought some new lips stick.

She had little money, but she felt obligated to make an impression on him.
He had tapped gently on her door. She was just applying the final touches to her face, she looked ravishing and he had remarked as such. He told her about his life. In effect he was a student, who did little studying. He was the wayward last son of an aristocratic family, with a huge family estate an hour from the city. He had various passions in his life, the principle one being sailing. She had shuddered when he told her this.

He failed to mention his love for woman, but maybe the woman he took to his room, were playthings, mild amusements to pass the cold winter nights. She felt humbled by him, all his stories, the grandeur attached to him. She came from such a simple background by comparison. When he had asked her to tell of her past life, she spoke of her husband. He seemed to be taking in each word, surprisingly attentively, she hadn't anticipated this. He had a frivolous side to him, but now she was seeing him in a new light, he was also a man of sensitivity. There was pity in his eyes. He had let her speak, without interruption. When she had finished speaking, he said how sorry he was, he was genuinely sympathetic. They had chatted long into the night. She had never had a night like this, the surroundings, the in depth conversations, his charm, his comprehension and sympathy.

As he drove her back, she anticipated he would try to lure her into his room. How would she react? Could she control the feelings she had for him, an aching desire for him. He hadn't, he'd soberly wished her goodnight. She had felt cheated. Maybe stories of her husband had proved un-alluring to him.   She heard him settle into his bed and she wished she was there with him. She had fallen into an unsettled sleep. Her husband had entered her dreams. He was proudly holding aloft, a large fish, it could have been a shark. His colleagues were lauding him. Suddenly the fish came alive, it was gnawing at his face. He was grappling to get it off screaming in agony, but when he did his face was flawlessly perfect, in fact he was laughing, his eyes shining like reflection of the sun on the sea.

She groggily made her way to the communal bathroom.

She opened the door. There was somebody in there washing his face. It was Oliver.

She apologised, as she had startled him. He had just laughed. She explained she had woken up after a bad dream. Oliver seemed to take everything in his stride. He also had woken up. Suddenly he pulled her towards him. They kissed urgently in the bathroom. He led her to his room. She just let herself go, she gave herself to him, she was no longer a sad widow, she was alive again and with a man she could never have imagined. Her head was spinning.

Their relationship flourished. He seemed to want to spend his time only with her. He even invited her to meet his parents. A long weekend in splendid surroundings. She had nervously accepted.

What would his parents make of her? She had come from such a simple background, fishing folk. His parents seemed pleasant enough. She hadn't dwelt too much on her background. In fact they seemed to quite welcome her, the woman he had previously brought to the family estate had been vulgar and sassy, she by contrast was simple, sweet in fact. What's more she was a stunning beauty, who turned heads as she glided into a room. They reckoned she might be just the person to calm Oliver down, she seemed to have some sense. Their youngest son had caused them many an embarrassment, with his reckless lifestyle, anything or anybody that had a good effect on him would be welcome. Of course it was unfortunate she had such a simple background, but she was well groomed and these days even royalty married commoners.

Oliver explained the itinerary for the weekend. Saturday, they would go for long walks and take a picnic. Sunday he planned to go down to the lake, where he planned to use his brother's sailing boat. She flinched at the idea, but he seemed insistent. While he sailed, she could walk and mind the dogs, two large golden retrievers, both playful animals. Her eyes had looked mournful, sceptical, but he had decided, his mind absolute.

It was Sunday. The day was perfect, little breeze, a blue sky, the calling of wild geese on the lake, that looked so picturesque, so tranquil, so inviting. She had watched him prepare the boat, as the dogs mingled friskily. They had sporadically exchanged loving smiles. He had kissed her tenderly, before setting out in the boat. She watched as he drifted further away from her. She had brought a book with her and she passed the time by reading and keeping an eye on him and on the dogs. She felt calm and insouciant and it seemed like he was heading back to her. He had even waved, she could make out his happy face.

He was now within a two hundred metres of her. Suddenly she caught sight of a figure in the water, swimming powerfully, almost super humanly towards his boat, while Oliver was oblivious. The man had appeared from nowhere.

When the figure reached the boat, with his powerful arms, he began to violently rock the boat, until Oliver was thrown out, tossed into the air. She screamed, but there was nobody in the locality, they were in a remote part of the estate. The assailant swam towards Oliver, whose arms were flailing arms flapping about, and he put his strong arms on his shoulders, dragging him down under the water. She felt helpless, she could only watch what was happening. The lake was deep and they were too far away for to swim out to, what could she do anyway? The dogs began growling, like they had only just been alerted to the danger. The two men disappeared from her sight for what seemed like an eternity, surely by now sucked deep in the lake. They were gone. The lake remained still, while her mind was awash with deep shock, as well as guilt for blemishing her husband's memory. What was painfully clear to her was he'd returned to vent his anger.

I AM THE LAST OF THE IDRIS

It is 2096 and I am wandering ceaselessly on an endless journey. There is a world that is open to me, but I am last of the line, trapped in my own solitude, in this vast wilderness. I am an Idris, some might describe me as a beast, others a secondary lower echelon of the human race. My type were originally contrived in a laboratory, by scientists, my genes contain those of human genes as well as animal DNA. My species, of "hybrids" were genetically modified and designed for specific functions. We are a species enriched with speed and agility, both our thighs and arms sinewy, our frames tall and overbearing. We also have great stamina and could travel long distances swiftly. One observer said we "could outrun a thoroughbred stallion and still have energy in surplus." We also have great faculties of vision.

We were initially created as a slave species, to go to war on behalf of humans, the ultimate killing machines. Once trained, our type were sold for huge profits, as if we were some new kind of military hardware, our physical attributes far superior to those of humans. One scientist commented "This creature will help to end our wars" adding proudly "it will fight our wars for us."

After a time, we were deemed useful for other purposes. A smaller version was created and we began to be used as a kind of sophisticated pet. We were "the must have" accessory in any rich household. Female versions were later created, much smaller and softer in appearance, with large doe eyes, long flowing silky hair and the gentle feline movements. With this advancement, we were able to breed, amongst ourselves. We progressed as a species at a much faster rate than scientists anticipated, we surpassed all expectations. Our mental faculties grew rapidly. We were still essentially constantly monitored, initially incarcerated like animals in zoos, but as time passed, increasingly we integrated, and began to spread. Idris ghettos grew in all parts of the developed world.

We developed our own language, which most humans could not follow. We even began to acquire our own hierarchy. Progressively we followed human traits. One Idris complained "humans dominate and abuse us but we progressively want to be like them." I was of "noble" birth, and in my youth I was arrogant. My father and mother taught prudence, but I carried on with my lofty attitude, my recklessness. I even dared to infuriate humans.

The relationship between humans and their creation the Idris, changed one fateful day, when I was still young. An Idris fighter, inexplicably turned his weapon on his human commander, slaying him. This rogue Idris spread a panic wave among humans. The alleged perpetrating Idris was found and systematically executed as an example, but the furor continued long after. There were those among the Idris, who claimed, the Idris fighter had been the victim of torture and abuse, purely for the sadistic pleasure of human soldiers, well outside the limits of military regulations and protocol. He had taken more than he could.

Others said there had been no such shooting. This was a plot fabricated by certain members of the military, to find a way to discredit and then oust the Idris from the ranks of the military. They believed wars should be fought with real soldiers, not fabricated mercenaries.

Scientists put this action down to the "one off action of an individual Idris.
"A singular faulty part in an otherwise prefect batch." Such words were not sufficient enough to convince the human population. The trust that had existed, had been broken.

Some lamented, "the Idris are becoming dangerously independent, they are developing self-will, they will all turn on their creators." One man coined an expression "The Idris are simply growing too tall"

Humans on the other hand had grown too comfortable, some said apathetic. There was the Idris, to do their menial work. Factories were full of Idris workers, even offices had Idris workers doing some carefully designated bureaucratic tasks. Some said humans were even letting loose the shackles of slavery and some Idris such as my father were even profiting from their endeavors.

The Idris helped run the infra structure, while humans wasted away their lives with leisure pursuits. The societies among humans crafted over centuries, were breaking down, as people lost their work ethic and just slipped into a hedonistic whirl of slothfulness.

Some scandalous reports said male humans were even sharing their beds with Idris. There was an outcry of "bestiality" that the human race had reached its lowest level of depravity. Some said disease would result. Others warned if a human/Idris birth resulted, it would be an abomination. Some claimed they'd seen abandoned undersized Idris humanoids, all horribly deformed and disabled, a far cry from the perfectly formed, prototyped "hybrid" predecessors. Some inferred these were the sordid result of liaisons between Idris and humans.

When a man arrived at a hospital, naked, with his eyes gauged out, his tongue ripped out from his mouth, people concluded he had been with an Idris female. Such females were blessed with great beauty, long shapely legs, slender torsos and the reputation of a ravenous insatiable sex drive, which most human men could never gratify. The female form of Idris was not as genteel, as once imagined, its sweet looks deceptive.

The mounting mistrust of Idris coincided the Idris feeling increasingly abused by their human creators as well totally unequal despite their increasing contribution to the world. Huge metropolis cities were being built at a rapid rate, with aid of Idris laborers, while greedy human entrepreneurs sat back and counted their profits.

The Idris growth in esteem, from being just slave fodder, to a much advanced functioning species, meant they were now visibly less tolerant of human exploitation, some said they were starting to develop their own ambitions. The Idris had the know-how and some humans suspected the where with all to mount rebellions and indeed wage a war against the humans.

When a power plant was destroyed and all the workers and security guards killed, at first it was put down to a terrorist attack, but a darker possibility emerged, that the attack had been carried out by The Idris. Some of the dead had signs of strange mutilations. The consequences of this notion impacted strongly on the Idris. Many domesticated Idris were expelled from households. Many just helplessly roamed the streets, where they died of starvation or were hunted down by gangs, who either killed them out of revenge or tried pitifully to exploit them. Attacks on Idris zones began to become common place, as well as retribution, on the part of the Idris. When talk of a manufacturing of a virus aimed at "culling" the Idris began to circulate, my father began considering the precautionary decision to move our family to a safer remote part of the country.

Another new sinister development occurred, with looting of an abandoned bio-weapons laboratory, The Idris could now release a strain of smallpox that would devastate the human race, in equal measure. It seemed both parties were prepared to use weapons that would even destroy many of their own. It was now all about high stakes, there was no attrition.

Despite travel restrictions and strict curfews being imposed on the Idris, my father at this point in time still had enough authority to permit him to travel. Some Idris had labeled him as being too close to the humans. I was young at the time, so could not gage, how he was able to have attained certain privileges. He had been allowed an "education" not afforded to many

Idris, but one that would enable him to "carry out his tasks". The Idris were no longer limited, they had evolved and were now sophisticated, some Idris even called my father "cultured" others even "regal".

Our journey was still fraught with danger and my father talked of vigilantes roaming about seeking to kill any Idris they came upon. We also came upon armed Idris, who had looted military hardware. We saw power plants burning, banks in flames, government buildings billowing smoke. The Idris had formed a well-structured resistance. My father said there would fighting on every street, the Idris would kill many humans. There were no battle lines, the Idris ghettos would be destroyed, but the Idris had integrated even in the hearts of big cities. We saw the terrible consequences of an escalating war. I had never seen so much violence and destruction. Then there were the many refugees, many sick and dying, blank faces on the road to oblivion. There were mountains of corpses piled up in street squares, bleak testament to mass slaughter.

My father had spent time fighting with the military. He had distinguished himself, but had been allowed to melt into civilian life, as a reward for his endeavors. He was given a prestigious post for an Idris. My mother was even allowed to stop working in a factory and began a more gentle office job. My mother was highly attractive. So much so, that I had seen humans ogling her lustfully as she walked majestically down the street. We were effectively living as humans do, a comfortable existence, most civilized. The breakdown of Human and Idris relations was a disaster for us and would set us on the road of being "the hunted". We could never stay in the same place a long time, we had to move to protect our existence. We had to live a treacherous existence to continue to survive, where caves often became our refuge. Humans and Idris were at war even in the most remote of places, so we had to tread with care. The Idris were being hunted down and remorselessly slaughtered. I grew up in this cauldron of fear. Each day I had to learn a hard bitter lesson.

It was also a time for me to interact with nature, to discover its great bounty. Generally the Idris were creatures of the city, confined to where factories were located. Among an industrial sprawl, punctuated by pollution and industrial waste, this is where we resided.

My father took to our new fugitive existence easily. He had spent time holed up in Swat valley, fighting an enemy. To pass the long hours of darkness he would tell us a range of stories, to lift our spirits. He told stories he had learned, of an ancient race of peaceful human farmers, whose abodes had been taken by invaders. We were even some days lodged in their old abodes, deep unoccupied caverns, with rock paintings, painted with red ochre, adorning the walls. Such images bemused me, we the Idris had no such history, and we had no beliefs in higher beings. We existed, we functioned and we did not delve further.

We did not realize it, but tragedy was close at hand. It was a day in which the sun beamed down on the red earthed plains. We were moving with our usual caution, my father dictating each precise progression from one place of cover to another. We had become accustomed to the exclusive sounds of nature, that of the wind whistling or the sound of rain beating down, slapping on stones. Suddenly we heard the by now unaccustomed sound of humans, they had been obscured by some rocks and cactus vegetation. They seemed intoxicated, shrieking and cursing.

We had seen no traces of humans in a long while. I saw my father's body tense. We were open and exposed, at this point in time. We had to hope that we had not been noticed. When the din from the humans augmented, we realized we had been spotted. There was worse to come. The humans were equipped with long range, high powered riffles. Suddenly a shot rang out. My father and I were ahead of my mother, we were not so far from reaching a place with cover. There was a sharp sardonic cheer of celebration. A bullet had pierced my mother's leg. She was pulling up in agony. There was no time. If my father and I reduced our speed we would be liable to be shot, if we continued we had a chance of reaching cover. It was a cruel choice, but my father urged me to carry on to safety. We reached a safe point and once concealed, we were able to observe my mother. She was letting out an excruciating screaming sound, such a piercing sound I had never heard before.

The men seemed to be sickly, with terrible rashes on their pallid faces. I saw one lift his riffle up and then slam it into my mother's beautiful face. Crimson blood spurted everywhere. I could see the agony of my father's face. I knew a big part of him wanted to go to my mother's aid, to enact some kind of vengeance on this group of renegade humans, who were violently brutalizing on my mother, but he knew he would just be mown down. They were laughing at her helpless condition. She was now pitifully waling, sure in the knowledge that her life was now ebbing away.

We sped off into the safety of a dark cavern, before the final blow that would finish her off. My father did not communicate much, he was too much in grief. He was also blaming himself, for allowing the family to be exposed to this threat, but in my eyes he was blameless. In days and months of never coming across a human, we had just been incredibly unfortunate.

The days that followed were terrible. My father was deeply pensive, as well as extra vigilant. When he deemed it safe we had returned to the location of my mother's death. Her horribly violated body remained. Birds surrounded her, ravenously picking at her remains, I saw one pulling on entrails. The sight just made me sick and the horror of this ugly scene repulsed my father, in a way I could never have imagined. There was never any Idris precedent for burial in any ceremonial manner. My mother was just left in the vile unpalatable manner we found her. We moved away, deep in our thoughts. The humans had moved on. Maybe with the sickness they seemed to have, they themselves had died. My mother's death was just some pointless killing.

My father seemed to be reenacting the death of my mother, over and over again, in his mind. It was like he was torturing himself. I just could not find any words to console or indeed communicate with him. We moved with a kind of dense silence, coming between us. Where he intended to take me, I did not know. I suspected he just wanted to move away as far as he could from the place where my mother had been so needlessly slain. My father normally had the air of someone regal, but he was simply broken, his head and heart swollen with loss and pain.

I noticed other changes in him. He was not moving with his usual vigor, he was now labored. I tried to confront him on this. He shrugged off my questioning, making me feel impertinent for even enquiring. I heard him suffering at night, as we lay side by side under the soft glow of the night sky filled with stars. He was sick, it was undeniable. His strength was sapping away. Maybe this was psychological, my mother's horrendous parting had made his life unbearable or maybe he had simply succumbed to some sickness. A thought pained me that he had conceivably brought this upon himself. There was the red flowered cactus, in the vicinity, he could have administered some of its lethal poison. He said strange things to me and at times I had the impression he was rambling.

Later he laid bare his situation, "I'm dying" he said, his head bowed, his face creased with pain. The words hit me harder than I could imagine. I wanted to disbelieve them, discount them. I wanted to imagine that none of the recent events had ever happened, that we were this Idris family roaming together, in the plains, in this red landscape, a complete family unit.

"You have to go on," he implored. He made me make a vow. It was a vow to try to survive at all costs. "You are in perfect condition" he told me. His own condition seemed to be deteriorating rapidly, perspiration dripping down his face, he was feverish. His last words to me, indeed the last words I would ever here from any living being were, "there's whole world out there for you." He sunk into a gentle coma. I found it hard to sleep. I felt if I did, he would slip away further away, leaving me. The moon spread its silvery light. Insects buzzed and droned. The air began to chill. Slowly I drifted into a dissatisfying slumber.

When I woke up, my father looked motionless and rigid. He had a particular look on his face, like he had arrived at a destination, after a long arduous journey. But the truth was, he had arrived only at death. I hardly dared to touch his stiff looking body. He had a rather grey pallor, Flies were hovering expectantly above his head. I pathetically tried to swat them away. "Father" I called out, breaking the silence. Of course he did not stir, his expression stayed fixed. I began to beat my forehead with my hand, as if I was chastising myself and I kicked the dusty ground in anger at his passing. I couldn't help myself from letting a loud piercing scream, that made birds scatter in fear. "Wake up father" I kept wailing, monotonously until I could not produce any more sound, my throat hoarse and parched. I could hear his voice resonantly in my head. "I'm dead and you have to move on."

I decided to cover him, he deserved dignity. I picked up the red dusty soil and sprinkled it over him. It took me time before he was even remotely covered. His limp corpse was still so gargantuan in stature, those godlike limbs that carried him at high speeds, his presence could not easily be obscured. I found some leaves which I added to the mound, that was once my regal father. I at least had managed to attain some kind of serenity. I wandered away, head bowed, deep in thought. I found a new location, which I deemed safe, not so far from where my father lay. Though I was extremely weary from my previous restless night, sleep did not come easy, my mind being too occupied. The wind was strong and disturbing.

I woke up aching and feeling desperately solitary. Before I could do anything, I felt bizarrely drawn to the place where my father lay. As I got closer, I saw a large bird of prey. Its piercing eyes stared at me for moment. I made a violent gesture towards it and in one quick swoop, it flew away. The wind had been strong and cruel and had dislodged all the earth I had tried to pathetically cover my father. His image was now even more grotesque. Scorpions and many other types of insects crawled liberally all over his body, parts of him seemed to have been gnawed at, by wild animals. His expressive eyes that had always sparkled during his lifetime had been gauged out, leaving gaping holes in his eye sockets. Some bird had no doubt feasted upon them. His color was now a mixture of dark murky grey and a dirty green olive color. I was filled with revulsion.

I wondered why I had returned, I should have known that nature would scavenge from him, show no remorse or spare him any dignity. I turned and ran, but I couldn't disperse his image out of my mind. I had seen humans mourn their dead. Women with tears streaming down their faces. Strange words I could not relate to, uttered solemnly. The Idris never were touched by religions or philosophies. We had no means to deal with death. I was lost and in mental anguish, the likes of which I had never experienced, my parent's lives wiped out within a short interval. I would have to hunt and feed myself. I no longer had my father's guiding hand. I felt confident I could survive in this large wilderness, but I had this prevailing fear I would suffer more from the extremity of my solitude.

As I wandered on, I saw no signs of either Idris or human life. I even stealthily ventured into the outskirts of once vibrant small towns, but there was no signs of life, just remnants of what had been. Some nights I heard the sounds of twigs breaking and imagined footsteps were approaching. However these were the sounds of wild animals foraging or tricks of an inventive mind. Each morning seemed like a window of opportunity, a possibility to find another being. Each night as darkness closed, the unyielding fact, that there was nobody, the war and disease had seen to this. The final epitaph had been written and sealed. I am forever pining for some kind of contact and this will never leave me. I have so many thoughts filtering through my mind, I needed another to help all my mental conflict. How I miss the companionship of my father and mother. I do have one source of comfort, a dog, which proves to be a loyal, protective and devoted companion. It seemed to follow me, attaching itself to me and before long we were fellow travellers. I am the last of the Idris and I promise to keep the vow I made to my dying father, I will continue to sustain my existence, in this bleak and empty world. When I die the brief heritage of the Idris will die with me, there will be no heir to the wide inheritance of this earth.

ANGEL CHILD

I had been woken up, by the sound of wailing. Such sorrow emanating from next door. It was my neighbor I presumed. The sound of such melancholy prevailed in my head, relentlessly. I had only seen my neighbor from afar, she was a blurred image of beauty and turbulence. Added to this terrible noise, I began to be aware of smell of burning wafting into my room. I bolted upright. I wrestled with putting on some clothes. I frantically banged on my neighbors door. With all my force I kicked open the door. I was confronted with a thick blanket of smoke.

I wrapped my shirt around my face, as a meager form of protection. The sound of hysterical crying was coming from behind another door. I foolishly tried to open this door. I reeled in agony on contact with the door handle, my hand severely burnt. I managed to catch the vague sight of a figure in white, consumed in thick white smoke. The wailing sound was curtailed and tranquility prevailed. Defeated by the smoke, I left the apartment. I took time to compose myself. There was a mounting sorrow welling up, at failing to save this woman, as well as a sense of urgency to alert others of the urgency of the situation. "Fire" I screamed in a hoarse fraught voice.

I heard a few doors opening, a few exasperated sighs. An old woman shuffled out of her apartment, looking dazed and confused. As the realization of the situation began to take hold. parents desperately ushered their bleary eyed children towards the stairs. Panic started to grip the building. I grabbed a bag from my apartment.

The stairwell was starting to get clogged up, with families frantically trying to get out of the building. I heard a voice. It might have been telepathic, a voice in my head, it was ticklish and soft, the voice of a child. "Water" the voice said in this temperate tone. I turned around. The child was dressed in blindingly white dress. Her hair was curled and blond, her eyes sparkling blue azure. For a moment the excruciating pain of my hand disappeared. I reached into my bag. I happened to always carry a bottle of water. It was probably a few days old. It didn't matter, she let out this delicious smile and cupped the bottle in her gentle hands. "Where are your parents"? I demanded. She looked like a child that was on her own, forgotten by the rest of the world, on her own in this time of need. She didn't answer, her face remained inanimate and serene. Suddenly I was jerked forward. A large man with a ruddy face, snorting, jostling to make it down the steps. "We want to get out of here mister," he bellowed. His wife nodded in accord, reinforcing his statement.

They both looked dehumanized, their faces white and severe, crazed looking. A melee of other people swept me further forward. The child was lost from my vision, but not from my thoughts.

Fire fighters were on the scene. A man with a hose trying to make his way in the opposite direction of the crowd. "Let me through" he shouted in gruff officious voice, to the residents so intent on getting out. I reached outside. The cold night air hit my face. The street was awash with activity, parents huddled closely to their children. I searched intently for the young girl, but she was nowhere to be seen and nobody knew of her whereabouts or indeed who she was. I was shepherded into an ambulance.

My time in hospital was long and arduous, my hand injury horrific, my hand now horribly disfigured. The pain was significant, coupled with the fact that in a matter of days I was due to get married. My future wife was away, visiting some relations. She was now due to marry a man with a grotesque looking hand. How she would react? This would surely test our love. My moment of attempted heroics or perhaps folly had meant my hand would never be fully functional, even withstanding many operations and physiotherapy, the doctor had painted, such a gloomy picture. As I was making my way home, I was fearful and indeed despondent. I had been pumped with drugs to alleviate the pain. I had no inclinations about what I would find when I finally got home. The building seemed to be back to normality. People sleeping soundly, after their broken sleep. I trudged upstairs. My neighbors door had been boarded up. There was a distinct smell of smoke, but the fire had been put out abruptly and proficiently.

I went into my apartment, managed to take off my clothes, with my one able hand, wincing with the occasional shots of pain. I finally put my weary head down. After a short while, I was drifting off asleep. When I woke up, my mind was filled with images of the previous night. It was the face of the young girl, that dominated. My phone rang, it was my fiancé, I had almost obliterated her from my mind, less thoughts of my disfigured hand, and how she would react. She spoke with great enthusiasm, up to the point, she detected, there was a big problem my end. Her voice dropped. "What's the matter"? she demanded. I had to explain all the events of the previous night. "Oh my God" she spluttered. I explained that my hand was now bandaged up and was not in a good condition. She had cooed at my attempts of rescuing my neighbor, heralding my bravery, but the mention of my hand had taken the shine off the conversation.

Walking down the aisle, to a man with a bandaged hand, on what was to be the

greatest day in her life, had limited appeal.
"Won't it heal" she asked in a displeased voice.
"I am afraid not" I said philosophically, with a
voice of stark resignation. I put the phone down
feeling somewhat let down. The wedding
seemed of weightier importance, to the fact that I
had a horrifically burnt hand. I called work to say
I would not be in, explaining the severity of my
injury.

I then drifted in and out of an uneasy
sleep. I woke up finally to the sound of muffled
voices. As slowly came around, my interest
mounted. It was apparent that the conversation
was between a fire officer and a policeman. I
managed to get some clothes on, withstanding
some pain. I opened my door. "I am her
neighbor" I said. "Her neighbor" muttered the
policeman incredulously, lifting an eyebrow.
"The woman who died, I was her neighbor". "We
found no body" said the fire fighter, with a
flippant voice. "What are you saying" I
demanded, "I saw her in the smoke, I tried to
rescue her." The two men laughed mockingly.
"This apartment has been empty and derelict for
years, there was a small fire, but nothing too
significant, probably some old wiring, our boys
had things under control in no time." I felt
indignant , as well as confused. "So you found
no body", I reiterated in desperation. The
Policeman, who had a huge snout of a nose, and
a derogatory demeanor, ridiculed "what a dark

mind you have, sir" He followed his comment with a scornful laugh, which was accompanied by the fire fighter, whose face was lit up with mirth. It was like the two were in collusion, undermining anything I said,

I returned to my apartment, slamming my door with venom. After a while the voices from outside, drifted away. The two men sauntered down the long flight of stairs, still ridiculing, sardonic cackles interspersed. I felt angry. I spent the day recovering and trying to take my mind off the pain of my hand. I asked some of the other residents if they knew of the young girl. Nobody seemed to know anything, I was met with blank looks. Even though I tried to give as full a description, as I could, I got nowhere. Nobody equally told me anything of the apartment and my "neighbor".

"The apartments been empty for as long as I can remember" said one old lady. "But I saw this woman on a number of occasions, just through the door" I protested, "I saw her last night.". The old woman moved shakily away, muttering, probably deeming I was insane and deluded. I watched some mindless television, but my mind was too agitated, to digest anything. I tried to sleep, it was impossible. I had curiosity dictating my thoughts, never relinquishing. I got up, almost mechanically, unsure what I was about to do. The answers to this mystery, lay next door. I slung on some clothes and went out of my apartment. Momentarily I looked at the apartment, that had a notice "Police notice keep out". As with my folly of the previous night, I decided to make a bold move. I re-entered my apartment and picked up a crowbar. With my one decent working hand, I managed to prise open the door.

The apartment seemed empty, cold and vapid. I held my arms close to my chest and shivered. I felt like an intruder. I began to question my own actions. What I wondered had led me to break into this latent apartment, which seemingly had nothing for me. I was about to turn on my heals, when I felt a presence. She appeared so suddenly and deftly . She looked miniscule in the vastness of the apartment. She glided towards me, she had a blithe look on her face. She was wearing the same immaculate white dress. She did not speak, I would not have expected her to, her face expressed it all. I pitifully tried to communicate with her. "What's your name" I asked in a soft voice, worried I might alarm her. She looked right through me. A smile reached her face and she seemed to enact a dance movement, she twirled and then giggled, her arms cutting an arc shape through the air. Any question I asked was met with total insouciance and disregard.

Her dancing became emphatic, she began to circle me, dancing round and around, to the point where I began to be mesmerized. My legs began to give way. I was blinded, a bright light seemed to illuminate the room. I was now a crumpled heap on the floor, my body immobilized. Something miraculous was happening and I was the beneficiary of this magic.

The young girl lent over me and unraveled the bandage on my hand. I did not protest. She was so gentle and proficient in the way she went about things. She was still smiling and joyful. Once the bandage had been unraveled, she held my hand. There was no pain however. Indeed any pain I'd had previously was now alleviated. I drifted off and went into a deep sleep. When I came around I was alone. I felt a bit groggy but as the grogginess began to wane, it became apparent a big change had happened. My hand was as it was before the fire, perfect without a single blemish. I gave the apartment a closer inspection. It was now back to this imposing emptiness, the child having disappeared.   There seemed nothing of value. Under a dense film of dust on the mantelpiece, there was a photograph. It had faded in time, but the resemblance was most apparent. The photograph was of a young woman, it was obviously the young child, some years on, having matured as an adult There was still the discernible beauty , but there was also some sadness engrained in her face. The young child was joyful and optimistic, the adult version, tainted by angst. I had encountered the optimistic one. Something significant had taken place, in her life, the bright glowing child had been lost to the world, or had it? It seemed like the glowing child had the capacity to rematerialize.

I took the photograph and went back to my apartment. I took stock of events, made some telling decisions. I put my impending marriage into perspective. I came to the decision I could not commit to a marriage, where I was unsure I would be loved. My confidence in the union had been broken, her love for me superficial, her reaction to my disfigured hand, had proved as much. I was cowardly in the way I broke the news. The fact that my hands were both in a perfect state, also besmirched me further. I skirted around all explanations, I would never have been believed anyway. I had left my now ex-fiancé weeping, great sobs, her head in her hands. I felt terrible, maybe there had been some love between us, I had underestimated her. I lived in almost solitude. I was trapped, unable to think beyond those events and the angel child, as I had named her.

What had happened previously in the apartment, was hidden in a veil of secrecy and I imagined deceit, none of the residents would let me in on the secret. I even had to question myself about the events of the fire and the days that followed. After all my hand was now in a perfect condition, with burns or marks to show, evidence that I had entered a burning apartment. I had no name, just images in my mind, images that would diminish in time. The residents of the building ostracized me for daring to question them, to probe into the deep mystery of what had passed in the apartment next to mine. There would never be any explanation, my mind would be in darkness.

A few years on and with the value of local property escalating, the boarding around the door were taken away. Some property developer had purchased the property and was investing money into it. In time so doubt rich owners were installed. They seemed friendly enough. One day the door to the apartment, was slightly ajar. I was sure I could make out the image of a young girl with a mop of thick curly blonde hair dancing with a scintillating smile of contentment, on her angelic face, it must be the angel child, but then again…

Francis H. Powell

FUNERAL TIMES

The air was thick with incense. The church dank
and musty. The congregation huddled together,
like sheep in a blizzard. But there wasn't a tear in
sight, dry eyes one and all, as I surveyed the
scene from my vantage point, in a different
dimension, being not among
them, not least in a physical sense. Seemingly I
had died. How did I die? I couldn't be objective
about this, I had no clues. There hadn't been an
epidemic of any kind in recent times, business
had been brisk, but not that brisk, and I should
know, as I was the director of a large funeral
emporium. All I knew I was that I was witness to
my own funeral.
There was the diminutive Pere
Jacques, presiding over the service, a man I must
have spoken to many times concerning funeral
details, those of other people's funerals. A man
whose monotone voice rarely wavered. It had a
soporific effect on all those who encountered it.
Sitting in the front pew was my wife,
Aude, a rosary clenched tightly between her bony
fingers, a black lace shawl covering her face, that
was slightly angled forward.
Close to her was my much beloved daughter
Chantal. I imagined of all those gathered, she

would be the most likely to show some kind of outpour of emotion, as she was the most susceptible to floods of tears, as she had done from the moment of her birth onwards. It was clearly apparent that this day, she was unquestionably calm, with an expression on her face that verged on boredom. Resting oblivious, in deep repose, cradled in her arms was Adeline her daughter. Normally this infant could match any child with her shrill scream, Many a time I'd seen her with tears gushing from her eyes, her pupils like large glistening black olives, accompanied by that scream, enough to make even the most unshakable person shudder.

There was of course one notable absentee, my errant son Gaston. If word of my demise had reached his ears, he would most likely be in some seedy bar, slumped over a drink, toasting his preconceived inheritance. I had tried to welcome him into the business. I had taught him the art of embalming, he'd even shown signs of a talent for embellishing the dead. When I suggested he would have a rosy career in the business, his reaction took me by shock. He looked me square in the face and said "I don't want to work with the dead, I want to indulge with the living." The next day he was gone, along with whatever cash he could pilfer to travel the world and no doubt every bar therein.

In the second row, her face looking ruddy, her hair somewhat unkempt, stood my wife's sister Angelique, her eyes drifting around the church, but never towards the box where my body lay. As I focussed on her, a twinge of sentimentality and guilt surfaced, as my heart had truly been with this woman, Angelique, the more gregarious of the two sisters, but my head had ruled Aude would make the suitable wife, for a person of my position and the sombre profession I had chosen.

In brief each member of those congregated for my funeral seemed to be screaming out the same message, loud enough to rattle even a dead person…they simply had little lament for my parting. I wouldn't be missed. I had obviously made a limited impression on each and every one of them.

There were notable irregularities throughout the service. The pall bearers had been badly arranged by Brevett, my successor, who obviously lacked my eye for detail. Consequently I was carried on an awkward slant, the floral display nearly toppling over. The organ music had sounded listless, sometimes drowned out by some heavy coughing and some inept singing that had accompanied it.

The priest had managed to confuse the length of years of marriage with my length of time in the mortician business, as he recalled my life, almost like a military roll call. When Adeline finally came out of her deep sleep, she exploded, needless to say, bawling her head off, but not for me, more for her mother's milk. Chantal had taken her prompt and had left the church, striding out the church without so much a quick glance back at the box where I lay, candles dripping and hissing around me.

There were so many things I could fault about the service, the new apprentice I had recently taken on, Privett, had almost fallen over, I suspected he had come to work on the back of a heavy drinking session, testing Brevett, to see how far he could push him, such subordination would never have happened under my tight reins.

Time seemed to speed up and before I knew it I was being unceremoniously hoiked, out of the church, in the direction of my final resting place, a plot of land I had reserved a long time before, with quite a sizable grave stone, I anticipated to soon mark the spot. The pall bearers were all out of step and so undignified. Chantal reappeared, Adeline now becalmed. The priest was saying a few erudite words to those who cared to listen. I was lowered down into the pit that had been dug for me. I focussed on the faces that peered downwards at the sodden turf. Chantal mechanically handed Adeline over to her husband, Adeline looked back her with a pitiful face, longing for her mother to reclaim her. Aude picked up some soil and was the first to jettison it, into the pit. It hit the wood with a thud, I felt. Chantal somewhat nonchalantly cast some more

soil on my coffin, still no signs of any obvious
emotion or grief in her face. I imagined I was
going to be engulfed in darkness that I would
soon be in a dense encompassing silence.

I was reconciling myself to eternity and
all it meant, when I heard a distant voice, one I
had never heard before. "He's not dead". This
was followed by an accompanied chorus
reiterating "he's not dead". From being in a state
of lull, I was starting to feel a transformation,
topped with a terrible physical pain, emanating
from my head. The "he" that had been referred
to, was me.

I was obviously the focus of a crowd's
attention. I could feel blood pumping at speed
through my body, as I become ever increasingly
invigorated. I had the feeling I was on a cold
damp road, as onlookers surrounded me. I was
not sure of what to make of my new condition.
From being what I thought to be dead, I was now
possibly going to have to reconsider the reality of
being mortal. I had obviously been in some kind
of accident. My body now energised, conscious,
I forced myself to take in my surroundings. I
managed to get my eyelids open. I could make
out papers, my papers strewn over the road,
including a copy of The Funeral Times. There
was an inordinate trickle of blood from a sizable
head wound. Had I been attacked? Some kind
of hit and run crime. Quite a crowd was
gathering in my honour. There was certainly

more feeling than what I had thought as being my funeral.

Then all of a sudden, through the narrow slits of my eye lids I caught sight of a familiar face. A woman running at speed, in some kind of desperation, towards me. It was Chantal, with concern etched on her face the wind lifted her long dress, her hair was ruffled and flowing. "Father" she cried out, in a despairing voice. "Oh my god, father". She put her hands to cover her face as she began to cry uncontrollably . Large globules of tears smacked onto my wounded head. "How could this have happened" she wailed. I was still in no position to communicate. I was not in complete control of my body yet.

As the sun came out, a funeral parade nearby, passed on, to the beat of a slow drum, but it wasn't my funeral, I was alive.

Francis H. Powell

BEHIND THE WALLS

Nobody truly knew what exactly went on behind the imposing walls of Luther Van Kaltman's vast estate. Indeed it was open to much supposition. Certainly stories circulated thick and fast, around the village, that lay close to the Van Kaltman's sprawl of land. The Van Kalman's had been subject to much gossip over the centuries, so for this matter Luther was no different. Little of his private life was known. Some said he lived with two beautiful sisters, in a tight incestuous relationship. Some embellished this notion, by saying they were the daughters of a Count who had been enraged by the fact that his daughters had been "snatched away" from him by the iconoclastic Luther Van Kaltman.

These days Van Kaltman never left the vast walls that surrounded his estate and his servants would only fleetingly pass through the village, they were bound to uphold the utmost discretion, Van Kaltman's life and secrets were never destined to leave beyond the walls of the estate. There were those who talked of some rare disease that confined Van Kaltman, meaning he was never to leave.

Others spoke of Luther Van Kaltman never coming to terms with his father's death and the affliction that seemed to plague the Van Kaltman family. Some spoke of hearing screams that broke the silence of the night, of acts of cruelty, depravity and debased unspeakable acts. The dogs that lived on the state were known to howl throughout the night. Travellers arrived in the middle of the night, but never left .

It was an engaging raconteur Johan Koeman, who told the village of some of the things he had seen and heard. He wasn't a regular employee of the Van Kaltman family, but he had been given odd restoration work from time to time, or at least so he said, nobody had seen him ever do a stroke of work as he was more likely found in a local tavern, drinking and speaking the day away. Johan Koeman was an enigma himself, he just seem to suddenly appear, nobody knew where he lived, or if he was married or other significant details about his life.

He had friends, so he said, who were servants in the city, and stories filtered through, about Luther Van Kaltman. This meant he was had a certain kudos and took centre stage in the Tavern. It was he who spoke of the beautiful sisters and their father who had been involved with a bitter feud with Van Kaltman. It was bad enough that Van Kaltman could take away from him one daughter but both his sublime daughters, each as beautiful as each other was too much, for the Count. He ruefully lamented the wretched day his wife the Countess had invited the little known Luther Van Kaltman to one of the splendid social occasions, organised to find suitable "husband material" for the divine Valentina, a mere seventeen years old and her equally mesmerising sixteen year old, sweet Fleur.

There was little doubting Luther Van Kaltman possessed great looks as well as other attributes the other young men didn't hold. He had a swagger and confidence that the other men couldn't match. He had a more advanced mind, one that had to develop fast since the death of his father, when he had been forced to tend to the vast Van Kaltman estate. It seemed like both sisters had fallen for him in equal measure for his undoubted charms. He had incessantly danced with both and it wasn't long before he was holding, not one but both of their hands, sitting comfortably unabashed between them. They were at a young and impressionable age and had throughout their lives shared whatever gifts came their way.

Some said pure greed ran through Van Kaltman's veins.

As well as a fine dancer Van Kaltman had proved capable of crafting letters talking of his love for both Valentina and Fleur in tandem. It was obvious that both girls were enraptured by him, they spoke of little else, as if the rest of the world had become non-existent.

One night the Van Kaltman carriage had arrived.
The two girls had absconded, leaving an
inadequate letter of explanation to their parents.
The freely admitted they had left the family
home to be with Luther Van Kaltman. On
discovery of their absence the Count had sworn
to not only to swiftly get his daughters back but
also vowed to avenge Van Kaltman who had
brought dishonour to a noble family, embroiled
them in a potential scandal. The family was now
fractured, the Count's heart empty of all but
remorse.

   The Count had a son and heir, but he
was both frail and weakened by constant
sickness, confined to hospital beds and in need of
constant medical supervision.
Though not a religious man, the Count still
believed in a certain propriety and it was a most
discomforting thought that his two daughters no
doubt shared the same bed of Van Kaltman. Their
innocence and virtue now lost, their chances of
finding a suitable match, virtually lost. Two
sisters "living in sin" sharing their affections with
one man, was unspeakable in "polite" circles.
The Count seemed to dissolve from society life,
shy away from any social events, there were
those that said once he had reconciled with the
fact he had lost his daughters for ever, he had
drunk himself to an early grave, but there were
no announcements in the papers to this effect

There was talk one night of sightings of a fine impressive horse drawn carriage parked by the grand gates of the Van Kaltmen estate. Johan Koeman had later spoken of a desperate man, a stranger with breeding, a Count no less who had come with a mission, he wanted to reclaim his daughters, to return them, back to the city, back to where they belonged. He had announced his himself at the gates and had been rebuked. He had demanded to meet Van Kaltman "face to face" he even condescended to allow Van Kaltman a chance to show a "modicum of honour and decency". Van Kaltman had given his servants strict instructions, which they always carried out to the letter, without exception. One of their primary instructions was to never permit any visitors within the walls, unless they had a "formal invitation". The Count had not been invited.

The servant's curt words had both bemused and irritated the Count greatly. Nobody but nobody had ever spoken to him in such away, not even in his short time in the army, had anybody imposed rules or curtailed him. It was he who dictated to others, not the other way round. Such insolence, he had wielded his whip and charged towards the entry of the gate, but had soon been soon been easily stopped, disarmed and told politely to leave. The rain began lashing against his face, converging the tears that streamed down his pained features. He began to wail the names of his daughters. "Valantina" "Fleur" he kept shouting, until his voice was so hoarse, it was now inaudible.

It was all futile, in any case his voice had been lost, recoiling off those walls that shut the outside world out, walls that contained many secrets. Van Kaltman had never appeared and no doubt had no intention of doing so, he was more than likely oblivious, to any kind of commotion. The walls had an imposing fortress effect.

The Van Kaltmans were an extraordinary family, whose misfortunes were better kept from the outside world. There was a well versed story that had been passed down through time and often mulled over in the village, that family had been cursed by one of the mistresses of Luther's ancestors, the philandering, Morten Van Kaltman. She had thought she had had won his heart. She had after all just delivered him a son. She had one day chanced on Morten suckling the breast of the young "wet nurse".

Such was her anger, with her considerable wisdom of the occult she had cursed Morten Van Kaltman's eyes. Within a short period of time he started to lose his sight. A sporadic line of blindness, afflicting the male line started to be established. Luther's father had suddenly been struck down by blindness. This coincided with Luther's birth. The two events connected in his mind. His resentment and cruelty towards Luther had made Luther's childhood painful. Luther suffered a severe repression at the hands of his father. His father would whip him. For the most minor of faults. His whippings would be ever stronger. Given the fact his father couldn't see the pain and anguish written on his son's face, he could only hear his son's cries to stop. His death had been somewhat of a release for Luther. Luther also started to recognise the value of his sight but also started to lavish and indulge himself with beauty, because at any point he might lose the faculty to see such beauty.

Stories such as Johan Koeman's brought a deep division among the villagers. The pragmatic doctor Lars Rickman often stared into the fire, impassive, his face not giving away his true thoughts. Nobody apart from Koeman's drinking cronies could support Koeman's stories, because nobody had set their eyes on the beautiful sisters. However they still listened attentively to what Koeman had to say, he told a good yarn whatever. The life in the village was generally dull and mundane, pages on the calendar turned over, but nothing of substance ever filled them, except the stories surrounding the Van Kaltman family. Then all of a sudden people started to note changes in Johan Koeman. He seemed to get ever increasingly clumsy and less assured. At first it was put down to his excessive drinking. But he would walk into

things. He seemed to use the utmost of concentration to perform simple tasks. It was like watching somebody feeling in the dark, careful steps, even to get to the bar. If anybody asked of his wellbeing, his face would light up as ever, but all could see it was just an act, to mask an underlying more serious problem.
"I'm fine, as right as rain, why ask."
Even the usually heartless butcher called Sven Kroneberg had questioned him. He had answered him angrily.
"Kroneberg , we are in a bar, not place to discuss my health, now drink up."
The butcher had sighed and then drew on his clay pipe, his face unconvinced at Johan Koeman's bravado. Kroneberg had looked at Doctor Lars Rickman for some kind of support, but not a muscle on the impervious Doctor's face had moved, it was like his face was made from granite. The doctor looked at Kronberg, just shrugged, but never said a word.
One summer's day, the heat unbearable, farmer's harvesting their crops, Koeman had started drinking early in the Tavern. It was nearly one o'clock and the Tavern was starting to fill up. Suddenly a carriage drew up next to the Tavern. The driver dismounted and opened the door to the carriage. Two smartly dressed young women stepped out. They were almost identical, the same height, hair colour, an obvious family resemblance. Both were

exceptionally beautiful. They were wearing pristine nurse's clothes, somewhat bulky given the fact that it was such a hot summers day, perhaps they were concealing something?

The men in the Tavern stared at them, as they slowly approached the Tavern. They walked awkwardly into the bar, obviously they were not on a social visit. They had come to see somebody in the Tavern, on a medical matter, but who?

Their eyes fell on Johan Koeman and they headed in his direction. One of them whispered something in Koeman's ear. He looked startled but, didn't react immediately. The other woman reiterating more firmly what had been said before.

"Come on now, you have your appointment with the specialist." Their equal concern mirrored each other, transmitted through the same beautiful blue eyes.

Koeman muttered something, as one of the young woman gently took hold of his arm to escort him out. The men in the Tavern, couldn't believe what they were seeing. Koeman said nothing to them as the two young woman led him, in the direction of the awaiting carriage. He hadn't even looked anybody in the eye, they would have been only be blurs anyway, his head was bowed. When he was out of earshot, a loud furore started. Everybody added their point of view, all except Doctor Richman, who just picked away at his stew, melting into the background, silent as a grave.

It was to be the villages last sighting of Koeman. He had been a regular, almost a feature of the Tavern, breathing life into it, a source of information of Luther Van Kaltman. There was a major emptiness now, nobody could tell stories like he could. A few weeks past and it was a Saturday night. Doctor Rickman was as usual absorbed in his own thoughts. Sergeant Krantz, the village Policeman came in with an urgent look on his face. He tried whispering something to the Doctor, but his urgency meant he raised his voice enough for those nearest to hear.

"A terrible thing has happened on the Van Kaltman estate, said the policeman panting, you must come immediately." The tone of his voice suggested there had been a "death" or perhaps fatal accident. The Doctor's face looked un-typically concerned, like some he'd half expected had happened. He left at speed and collected his equipment. After he had left the Tavern came alive. The doctor had access behind those walls, some suggested he had been a regular visitor to the Kaltman estate, there were those who said he was party to information that could unlock the truth and satisfy their cravings for information. Some felt resentment to the doctor, who had retained his silence, he had often been among them and was now seen as a man of duplicity.

The Doctor's mind was centred on what he would find when he arrived at the Kaltman estate. It had been he who had been called to the scene of Luther Kaltman's death. He'd heard reports Luther Van Kaltman's fine mind was deteriorating, set off by the specialist's stark prognosis. Luther Van Kaltman, the doctor had concluded a long time ago was both genius interspersed with madman. He could dissect and adopt the mind and personality of another person, he had the skill of a great actor, he could metamorphose at will. Luther Van Kaltman had played games with the simple villagers, his real personality hidden behind a mask, of a character he had played with great craft. He had filled their minds with stories, which had worked well, because they had totally been distracted from the truth that lay behind the walls. Van Kaltman was keeping the village alive. If they had known some of the profanely insane patients secured in the infirmary wing of the Kaltman estate, his operation could be jeopardised. His work with these patients was specialised and delicate. Some of the patients had committed the most profanely evil depraved acts, and most citizens would not want such people on their doorsteps, in their midst, even with the knowledge that they were secured behind walls and under Van Kaltman's supervision, secrecy had been paramount. Van Kaltman himself however had been touched himself by a kind of insanity, coupled with the fact his sight was ever waning.

It was the Ritzinger sisters, Valentina and Fleur, who had broken the news of Luther Van Kaltman's chronic situation. He probably had a matter of hours to live, he had lost a lot of blood. The sisters who were used to dealing some of the severe cases that passed through the infirmary, and had worked closely with Van Kaltman, since they had graduated from medical school, were besides themselves with fear and concern for Van Kaltman's life.

The patient who had attacked Van Kaltman, was usually such a docile innocuous man. Of course he had long suffered from many delusions, but he certainly was classified as being a violent dangerous type. He had woken up with the sunlight streaming through into his cell. His mind was a haze. He had heard the voices of Fleur and her sister discussing some delicate matter. Their voices had formed a connection in his mind, or had triggered a dormant memory. He had started screaming, repeating the same words over and over again.

"You destroyed my father, you stole my sisters, Van Kaltman, Van Kaltman, Van Kaltman, I will revenge you." Van Kaltman had been summoned. When he arrived two burly men were restraining the patient. The man was protesting.

"Get your hands off me, he hissed, I am a Count, how dare you, my father was Count Von Ritzinger, no less." The two male nurses had faces that said they had heard it all before.

Van Kaltman had told the men to let him go, he would deal with this situation personally. The patient was being out of character, he had been under Van Kaltman's care for a long time he was almost like a "family member". Van Kaltman calculated his soothing influence, would stabilise him, he had this effect on most of the detainees He had even told the male nurses to leave him. When he thought he had the man under his control, the usually feeble impassive man went for him, with some kind of brute force, that had been stored up over time. By the time the nurses had been alerted to what was happening it was too late. Van Kaltman could not have put up any kind of defence, being a virtual blind man, he would never have seen where each blow was coming from. The patient had managed to conceal a screwdriver in his mattress, which he had used as a weapon. The screwdriver had been lost by a careless worker from the city, who had been brought in to do some restoration work, a man who liked to talk. In fact he liked to talk too much and such bravura was unwelcome, he was dismissed and sent back to the city. Van Kaltman demanded discretion and efficiency from even his casual labourers and this man had showed neither attributes.

When patient had calmed down, it was like he had totally forgotten what he had done. He returned to his feeble, sickly self. His feud with Van Kaltman, all but forgotten. Doctor Rickman found Van Kaltman to be in a terrible state. His wounds were bandaged and he administered some morphine. Van Kaltman was still conscious, the Doctor sensed he had an enormous will power to survive, even with the odds stacked against him. Van Kaltman asked for the Ritzinger sisters. The Doctor had heard them gently sobbing in the adjoining room, their care for Van Kaltman more that "professional" Doctor Rickman watched as some kind of discussion evolved between the sisters and Van Kaltman. There was a conclusion to this discussion. A conclusion   that was to leave the doctor somewhat abashed . A priest was to be summoned immediately. Van Kaltman was to be moved to the family chapel. There was to be a wedding. Van Kaltmen was to marry Fleur immediately, her older sister had appeared aggrieved, but the decision had been made by Van Kaltman. The Doctor's vapid protests as to the inappropriate timing of a wedding were ignored. The heavily sedated and wounded Van Kaltman was moved from his bed, by the two burly male nurses.

In due time Father Shromfenburgen the village priest arrived. Father Shromfenburgen was confused, but readily agreed to perform the ceremony. How could he refuse a dying man's request?   There was no wedding dress, it had all been done out of some kind of necessity. The beautiful bride stood in front the of alter with her dying groom lying down, swathed in bandages. It had not been planned, it was done to preserve the Van Kaltman name. The sister's were to continue the Van Kaltman work. It was apparent to the doctor that both were with child, no doubt Van Kaltmen's child. The service was bizarre and Van Kaltmen would slip in and out of consciousness, his words feeble, barely discernible. Both sisters held his hand, imploring him to stay conscious, squeezing him to extract the necessary words, willing the conclusion to the ceremony.

A ring was put on Fleur's finger, a sweet smile reached her lips. By the time the service and formalities were complete, Van Kaltman was at death's door. It seemed like the "last rites" would be more appropriate. He was promptly taken back to the infirmary wing, the Ratzinger sisters both at his side. The doctor had been a witness. He was trusted by Van Kaltman. He had never questioned some of Van Kaltman's strange behaviour. He had never given away any secrets.

The Doctor was sure of some things, Luther Van Kaltman, should he die, which seemed highly likely, he had an heir, if not two. The Doctor also reckoned that when he finally returned to the village, he would be subject to a long weighty inquisition on the part of the villagers, in the Tavern. He wondered what he should tell them. He would have to concoct something of note otherwise a new sickness would spread through the village, killing them off slowly, one by one. With no more stories of Van Kaltman, they would surely die from a sickness known as "banality".

Then next day he set off nervously to the Tavern. He had left the Van Kalman estate, Van Kaltman was left in the care of the Ritzinger sisters and providence and the doctor had received no news, bad or otherwise. He could hear the din of the Tavern, quite some distance away. As he got closer he thought he recognised a voice. It was a voice of a raconteur. It went against all his medical knowledge, but the voice was teasingly like that of Johan Koeman's. If so he could only conclude some kind of momentous miracle had happened behind the walls. The Doctor increased his stride, and was even more inquisitive now.

Francis H. Powell

THE WORLD THERE AFTER

PART 1 THE EXODUS

It was while watching Zee Tube, the
second president of the new Global Republic,
make a chilling speech, to a carefully elected
few, that Mobatroy and Rad Meterman decided
to take action. Mobatroy had just become
pregnant.

"We will create a new existence,
nothing like anything we have known before
there will be no more human fallibility, no more
physical pain, we have long surpassed, what
those in the past called God, we will be the new
deities living in perfection, we are following our
destiny, we need purification and eliminate all
that can damage us in any way, we must follow a
process, a radical one, it is our brains that make
us function, our bodies are just dispensable, mere
receptacles for the brain, we must follow the path
to the final evolution, the final brushstroke that
completes a masterpiece"
He had continued. "Humanity has run its
course".
He said gleefully, "indeed only last week another
zone had to be shut down."

He raised his voice, "We must head towards an exodus, we have no more place on this world."
His voice had no traces of emotion.

The world was on its final journey towards being obsolete, humans with bodies were now an unnecessary inconvenience in President Tube's eyes. The world had become unsustainable.

A vast catastrophic event had seen a previously undetected "super volcano" erupt and now a dense cloak of ash shrouded the world. Large areas were bereft of sunlight, causing an eternal winter. Nothing grew now. All animals had died, in a short period of time. Famine and disease had spread and the world was now the most meagre of existences, threadbare and barren.

A pregnancy within the Republic was not only rare, it was virtually outlawed. The few woman that had children these days had decisions to make. Some secretly sold their offspring to rich people for vast sums of money. Others saw their children being snatched away from them by the authorities, no doubt either used for scientific purposes or simply exterminated. Some had them snatched by child traffickers, it was big business, children being such a rare commodity. The republic scattered the propaganda liberally across the world their slogans.

"Children = poverty"
"Think of the world, not another mouth to feed"
"Children spread disease"
"A smaller population is a better population"
It wasn't just children who were
being systematically weeded out, it was anyone
who did not match up to the criteria of those in
power.
"Do you merit your existence" in vast letters
was an often used slogan.
In truth however the world had been slowly
dying a lingering   death caused by apathy.
People had just fallen into submission or they
simply knew no better.
 Those of a scientific mind or intellectual mind
were safe, less they showed any signs of
subversion. For those lacking in required
intelligence, their survival chances were limited.
They were shipped away in their hordes, to lands
where there was no chance of any kind of
nourishment or kind of sustainable existence. It
was guaranteed, they would soon be killed along
with the others who shared their predicament or
fall victims to disease. Few parts of the world
were functioning. Countries had long since
ceased to exist. Indeed an entire continent had
been used as a dumping ground. Some said if
you flew over this land you would see vast white
mountains, stacked high with skeletons, that if
there was still sunlight, they would glisten like
candy. It was said that in the past this land had

been used for dumping prisoners, now it was for the diseased and for the dead.

Not only was the constant smell of death, language had also died. People spoke the same global language "world sphere" this language omitted words that had prevailed before in the old languages. There was no word for "farmer" there were no words such as "compassion" "equality" "socialism" "maternal". Most people only spoke prosaic sentences full of jargon, basic survival language.

All books containing references to any of the religions had been long since destroyed and possession of such books resulted in instant death penalty.
"In a word of near perfect technology, it is us who can define the afterlife" was a boast that was commonly circulated.

Hidden away Mobatroy and Rad Meterman owned such a book, it was called the "Bible". They were able to decipher parts of it, it made strange reading. It was surreptitiously passed onto them by a fellow scientist, just hours before he died. His name had been Elon Maki, his life had been a lie, as notes he had made, hidden in this "bible" revealed. There was more they discovered, infinitely more. Hidden away they had also an old device, that had not seen the light of day in many years. They had hooked it up, mostly out of curiosity, to find out what was stored in it.

They had been allowed to look over his possessions and acquire what they deemed of value. It took time for them to unravel this laughably primitive apparatus, but they were soon able to convert the files on its data base, into "mind files" which they downloaded onto their own minds.

It was like they were rediscovering the world again. The accessed information that had been forbidden to access. The history of the world mapped out. Languages which had died or been outlawed, were stored in archives. The ways people used to live, naturally primitive tin their eyes, but at least natural. "Life had so much color in the past" considered Rad. They found out how humans used to interact, how they expressed themselves, emotionally, sexually, and creatively, how they nurtured and loved their children, families and pets and animals. They had laughed and cried, in the past, unheard of in the grim bleak world they inhabited. They now felt something they had never sensed before, they felt "human". This feeling could be dangerous, if detected. It was obvious Elon Maki had kept up a pretense in the most meticulous way. This gave them the confidence to do things they had previously thought as unthinkable. The world they had learned about was full of in discrepancies for sure, but it had color, tones, flavors, shapes it was so rich.

Mobatroy and Rad Meterman were both part of the "chosen ones" on account of their unique neurological and technological expertise and their contribution to a new phenomenon that bring about the new dawning of mankind. It's name was the "Brainpod" it would be available to the select minority, but it would enable them to exist in a virtual heaven, their brains being preserved while being interfaced with computers, in a protective pod, designed to last into eternity. The brain would be stimulated in such a way it would be like living a normal life. Its ramification would be the necessity to put an end to mankind and it would be an existence only permitted for a select few, those living in the green area of zone one, the executives and scientists, those deemed worthy. "There has always been a natural selection process" lauded Zee Tube.

They may have been words accredited to him but would have been most likely contrived by "the committee". Zee Tube was an indistinctive face, the front for this "committee" a shadowy group of men, made up of top executives from the few industries that still functioned, in the North East zone. Zee Tube was purely of symbolic value, someone to hide behind, while they went about their ways, hidden in the shadows. Zee Tube was probably the half clone of the previous president, and certainly had no leadership skills or indeed what was in previous times described as political know-how.

"What would it be like to have a baby, a real child" Mobatrroy had mused. They question had hung in the air, like a large cloud about to burst forth with a storm. He had stared at his feet, at their grey standard carpet, that covered their sizable abode.

"That would be sheer insanity, more insane than some of the work we do" Rad had replied, in a hush voice, almost indignantly, like he had been wounded. It took time not only for him to be convinced, due to the inherent dangers, but also for Mobatroy to get pregnant. At first it was not a problem and they could move freely, but after a period of time, she was unable to see anybody or leave the complex where the two were privileged to live and work on their projects.

"For safety purposes and for the fulfillment of the project, it is vital we are afforded the utmost privacy, our work is most delicate, we require privacy at times, our work burden is heavy." Rad had informed a stark looking official, who had looked at him scornfully, but due to the eminence and value of such a scientist, he was forced to agree. "The brainpod will be our salvation, comrade" Rad had said, in an earnest voice.

They had always thrived on creating scientific breakthroughs but like

Elon Maki had obviously discovered they were spending their lifetimes creating a synthetic world, it would be no doubt a lot richer than the real world; the grim dust bowl that they knew, could not compare to the world that had once existed; A world bursting with diversity and genuine vitality. The previous world where things grew from soil, where humans interacted with nature and children were born out of love, a child was a legacy really worth leaving.

Elon Maki had been their mentor and had a great influence their rise to prominence.

"Scientists love to create, but not all we create is the benefit for all, we often serve the privileged and we have contributed to this sterile, world without any values, this will be my dying shame, the thoughts I take before my demise" He had scrawled on paper,

Along with other surprisingly well observed pieces of philosophical trains of thought, lodged in a bible that had severely begun to determinate, but still included many legible parts. Elon Maki, the top scientist of his epoch. Seemingly dedicated to all the work of the Global Republic, a supposed great advocate, but deep down a passive subversive and man who had gained access to how things once were. They had always been awe of this man. He had seemed such a clinical man. It seemed inconceivable he had always thought in the manner he had, with notes embedded in this bible, and the data he had preserved at such risk.

He had been described as the predecessor of Zee Tube, as being "the leading contributors to the rise of the new Global Republic".

"Look at the sky" he had once said to Mobatroy and a gathering of the vast scientific section in the sanctity of the green area, a massive protective dome, "it's grey, nature did this to us, we have to devise a world where nature, disease, can't destroy us ever again." It seemed such utterances may have been a ruse, as his notes also revealed regrets, for example regrets of never experiencing the warmth a child can give, of the fundamental pleasures of fatherhood.

This side of him was undetectable on the surface, as some of his research had gone to extremes and knew no ethical bounds. "We do what we need to do, to prolong a quality of life, we are instruments of the new Global Republic" He had said with an earnest face, "scientist's have a particular role in this new evolution, in fact we rule over all that shall be in the future, existence depends on us".

The committee had been for a long time drawing up plans for the "exodus"
Super transporters had been long been worked upon. Their destination would be Mars, which had the perfect conditions for the installation of

over five thousand *brainpods*, in a chosen
location. The electricity supply in the green area
and other surviving zones would be switched off
and no more artificial food would be produced.
Those left behind would perish in a matter of
weeks, from starvation and from the extreme
cold. It was a calculated move by the committee,
those they deemed as threats, the subversives,
would be liquidated. The list of the "Chosen
few" had meticulously been drawn up, by the all-
powerful committee members. Anyone who had
met their displeasure would be left behind, facing
certain death in a matter of time.

Rich industrialists who had pumped
money into the project, of course had their
places. Surgeons would be needed to perform the
operations, as well as technicians. They would
dock at "Gallactica," the vast space village,
where upon the landmark process of
transformation to paltry human beings with
human bodies to being ensconced in
"brainpods" would begin. "Man's final
triumph" trumpeted Zee Tube.
The final production of "brainpods" would be
round the clock and a fleet of transporters were
already being equipped and prepared for their
departure.

Nobody knew exactly how old Dag
Shnoor was. His body had been modified and
regenerated many times. His brain was full of
incredible knowledge of human genetic

engineering. In his time he had been a leading scientist in the new world republic, now his own brain had dysfunctions, it was full chips and faulty circuitry. He had a huge tumor growing compounding the problem. His brain was no use to the Republic, it could not even be put to use in the "brain bank". Consequently he became a leper, shunned by most people and now horrendously thin as he had been put on "rationing" a cruel insult, to a man who had gone past so many scientific frontiers in his time.

It was Dag Shnoor, who Mobatroy and Rad Meterman turned to when the fetus growing in Mobatroy was developed enough to take out of her womb to perform some vital modifications. They needed to tap into his knowledge. He had been surprised to be invited to their quarters, which was fully equipped as a laboratory. They had explained they were doing a delicate operation and needed his knowledge. He had been dubious but willing. He was soon like his old self, like he had been before when orchestrating delicate operations.

The fetus was modified in such a way, that it would develop at an incredibly slow rate, indeed it was adapted to reach full development a hundred years on. It would grow in a capsule, which Mobatroy had dubbed "the incubator pod". It was adaptation of another project, however it required a risk, to be able to access the vast stockpile of materials, stored away.

While going through the possessions of Elon Maki, they had discovered he had a device that could break codes, and open high security doors, and could get access in and out of the green area.

Also stashed away was voice changing material as well facial duplication material, with the capacity to replicate the exact features, of some the leading committee members. He had walked around freely and even the psychic police had been able to distinguish him from the alias he had adopted and that he was a double. Maybe he had even been in collusion with some subversives. Rad would use such material to good effect.

With fortune, and the help of genetic modification this child would be able to surface and exist in a world, which would no longer be shrouded in grey ash and pollution. It would be able to grow things to survive. They would even leave provision for it to reproduce. It had settled into its new environment, without complications. The incubator pod was laden with much equipment and monitors tracking the fetus's heart. It would be feeding off a highly nutritional liquid, with a drip. Apart from all the basic requirements fitted into this ovular shaped device, there was also a huge bank of knowledge, that once his brain was large enough, would be fed in slowly, so on full development, he would be full of vital survival knowledge.

Moving the "incubator pod" to its final destination, would be another risky procedure. They would need digging material, but firstly to get out of the green area, past the psychic police. The answer lay in changing their identities and commandeering a vehicle, using the identities of a committee officials. They would be able to change their thought patterns while passing the psychic police, so as no arouse and suspicions. Anyway the psychic police were far more preoccupied with those entering the highly protected green area, there was still a threat of terrorism and sometimes people tried forlornly to infiltrate, to increase their chances of survival, because the green area was the only place guaranteed to have food and other resources. On capture all illegal migrants were treated with the outmost severity, then disposed of, the risk of them bringing in disease was seen a great threat.

Skyrag Kay and Roog Britt fitted the profile of committee members who carried enough authority and whose voices and appearance could be replicated, as well as thought patterns. Both austere, they planted immediate fear into the minds of those who encountered them.

Turgig drove a transporter. He was a simple man, programmed only to follow orders and perform his job, he did not have the capacity to question. His brain could easily be scrambled. It was more the psychic police who would have

to be duped. Mobatroy and Rad had to
program the same brain patterns as the two
people, whose identities they had stolen, for
duration of the time of their departure from the
green area.
 He had a completed a long shift, when suddenly
he felt a firm tap on his shoulder. He turned
around and met the cold steely eyes of Skyrag
Kay, who was accompanied by Roog Britt.
There was a momentary silence before Skyrag
began to talk.
"We are commandeering both you and your
transporter for a military operation."
"I see comrade Skyrag" said Turgig.
"We have some material we need to install in
your transporter comrade" Skyrag said,
"come with us". There were many people
milling about. Some people politely nodded at
Skyrag, acknowledging him.
          Mobatroy and Rad, under disguise
had put the "incubator pod" into a wooden
freight and activated its defense field, making it
undetectable. It was on wheels and they
managed to wheel the freight to where Turgig's
transporter was situated. They carefully put the
freight in the back of the transporter and joined
the convoy, who were exiting the green area.
          They reached the barrier, where the
psychic police would no doubt be observing each
departure, noting any irregularities of thoughts.
The two people whose identities they had

assumed often made random journeys. The real Skyrag and Britt were involved in highly classified last minute meetings concerning the "exodus". The minds of Mobatroy and Rad were both now fully locked into the minds of those they were impersonating. Rug Dibbitz who normally could tune in immediately to any irregularities had been placed closer to where the Exodus was to take place and those in his place had not been programmed to match is standards. The Exodus area was now top priority. It seemed concerning the green area, extreme security had been replaced by mediocrity. The transporter was allowed to exit the green area.

Mobatroy and Rad were now able to lock out of the minds of Skyrag and Britt and now if there was no interventions, they would be able to complete their task.

Turgig was dispatched from the transporter.

"This transporter is needed for classified mission and we have to assume full control of it, you are dismissed comrade." Turgig's over programmed mind was at sea, without the power of reason. He had left the transporter, muttering words as if in a loop, "I just obey orders comrade, obey orders, I obey orders. " He was suffering from a terrible chronic malfunction, his brain going into meltdown. He had never failed to return to the depot before, but he had been programmed only to obey and in his mind if he was told by who he perceived to be comrade

Skyrag, he had no options. He had trudged away his hands gripping his head, looking on forlornly as the transporter sped away.

Mobatroy and Rad now had to now get to an area of what had been a forest. It would act as a place where the incubator pod, could be well concealed. The transporter they had requisitioned had the facility to dig through the snow that lay and the frozen ground. It would be dangerous still. What if the psychic police had latched onto them and were biding their time? There were also gangs that roamed areas such as the dead forest. Rad thought it prudent to set up a brain scrambler, once they had found the spot, where the incubator pod would be placed. They could not afford any unwanted intruders.

They entered the forest. There was a foul acrid smell that even permeated through the transporter. It was hard to navigate through the dead forest and they had some way to go before they could feel they had found a safe enough place to start the work to install the incubator pod. After twenty minutes of steering through the dead forest they spotted a secluded clearing which they deemed to be appropriate.
Firstly they needed to pierce the thick layer of ice that covered the ground. Once this was achieved they began to bore deeper into the frozen ground. They shifted the incubator pod out of the transporter. Snow began to settle on the ground. They had to make some last minute

adjustments and programming to the incubator pod.

Mobatroy looked down on the fetus, as if transfixed. The enormity of what they were doing had dawned on her.

"We should name this child before we place it in the ground" said Mobatrroy.

"It shall be called Adam" replied Rad. It was a name that had featured in the bible, the book that Elon Maki had concealed.

"Well Adam we will probably never see you again, but so much hope rests on your shoulders," said Mobatroy pensively.

"We need to hurry" urged Rad, defusing her moments of sentimentality.

The incubator pod was lowered gently down. Air ducts were placed to surface. The pod was covered with the displaced earth and finally with dead branches.

They had just about finished , when they saw distant lights. They raced to the transporter. The weather had now worsened and visibility was thin, but they had to get away, they were being chased. The transporter was not equipped to move at a high speed and there were many obstacles, for example machinery that had been discarded. In his back monitor Rad realized they were being pursued by Rug Dibbitz, in his patrol transporter which could get up to excessive speeds. They stood no chance. Their best hope was to abandon the transporter and then buy enough time to use a brain vectortron to erase huge pockets of brain matter, all traces of the incubator pod, indeed all their scientific knowledge. They needed to literally wipe clean their minds, to render them as the brains of young children. They leapt from the transporter and ran in the direction of a thicket, which Dibbitz's transporter would not be able to access. It would give them just enough time to reformat their brains.

When Dibbitz reached them, they were cowering and stared him with fear on their faces, the fear that children might show. He recognized a change in them. They were not their usual selves. He noticed the brain vectortron that Rad still cradled in his arms, like a child might a favorite toy. Dibbitz's features sharpened. He knew something momentous had happened, but he would be unable to extract data from their brains, they were in the latter stages of meltdown. Fury was welling up inside him. What was more the Exodus project would be delayed, as the final programming and adjustments still had to be made and comrades Rad and Mobatroy were the only two who could make them. It had extensively been their project, they had been left to their own devices.

What were Rad and Mobatroy doing? This disturbed Dibbitz greatly. He was just clocking off when he chanced upon a remark, by one of his subordinates, working at green area exit 501. "Skyrag Kay and Roog Britt" the subordinate had said "were on a classified mission and were in transporter 7z96.". This he knew to be impossible, as he had spent the day with Skyrag Kay and Roog Britt, he knew they had both been reassigned, to work solely on the "Exodus". It seemed to him impostors had hijacked not only the identity of Skyrag Kay and Roog Britt , but also the transporter. Having tracked down the transporter, which was closing in on the dead forest, he also picked up for a short while, the unlikely brain patterns of Rad and Mobatroy, the two most eminent scientists, so vital to the completion of the brain pod and the entire exodus project. Summoning some of his best men and women, he had raced after them. He had assumed they were in league with some subversives. Such people still roamed the dead forest and there was always the danger of some kind of infiltration into the green area and some planned atrocities and destruction.

Rad and Mobatroy's fear suddenly seemed to change to mirth and both began to laugh uncontrollably, as Dibbitz's men led them away, back to the green area, where some kind of futile investigation would be launched. Futile because with their brains now were close to being reformatted, they were useless to the Republic. Dibbitz would have the forest combed for subversives, but he felt unusually inadequate, he had no good news to report back to the committee, only some horrible truths that would send them spinning into anger, perhaps demanding his resignation.

Perhaps Rad and Mobatroy were laughing, due to the enormity of what they had done, a last flashback, a final reminder, before their memories would be blank and useless. They seemed triumphant, exuberant. Dibbitz had never seen them like this before. Strange for two people who had broken some of the Republic's most serious laws and were now liable to be punished in a lethal way.

By the time they reached the green area, any thoughts of what had happened in the dead forest and the time leading up to this event had vanished from their minds. The world was in its death throes, but unbeknown, lying in the ground, there lay some kind of legacy. Planted in the ground, like a seed, was what would surely be the last man alive. One last seed of hope.

PART TWO

TWO HUNDRED YEARS LATER

REGENESIS

"It's time". A message was implanted in his brain. It would take time for him to surface. His body was fully developed, but it had much to acclimatize to. The pod had opened and he had slowly maneuvered out of it. He felt the sensation of wet soil on his skin. It was a struggle, his body was strong, full of nutrients, but it was not used to moving, as he'd for long time only had limited movement in the pod. He had followed the direction of the air ducts. The pod had not been buried so deeply, but it was a struggle. When he got to the surface, he was panting. He was not used to real air. He opened his eyes and a strong burst of sunlight hit them. He winced. There was so much for him to take in. Colors he could never have imagined. The forest was simply full of color and animation. It took time for him to haul himself up, to stand on his feet, had been an enormous task. Years of being dormant, but now he felt truly alive.

He had been instructed about what he needed to do, once he had surfaced, but it involved a lot of endurance.

There were sounds he was unfamiliar with, as the wind, rushed through the trees. He noticed objects in the sky, rising upwards and then swooping down. His heart was beating fast, he was experiencing something, he had never through before, that of fear, the need to survive. On the ground green material grew, it was soft and luxuriant. Suddenly something fell from a tree. It was a round shape and a mixture of red and green. A word formed in his mind, it was "apple". He gripped this object, as if it was highly precious, indeed it was, for it was something that would sustain him, in the near future. .

Slowly he hesitantly began to survey the local environment. He felt loathed to be far from his pod, but he knew he would have to take some risks to survive and find ways of sustenance. He enjoyed the heat on his skin and all that he saw around him, which amounted to a kind of paradise. He had lived in his mind for so long and had not enjoyed the benefits of touch. He felt like touching things, to experience different textures and sensations. Some things he touched were not so pleasant, the rough bark of a tree, for example. He also started to develop a strong sense of smell. There were flowers amongst the thick carpet of grass. They emitted different smells, each one a new pleasant experience. He spent a long time just taking in his new environment, but as he did so he began to notice, the sun was not as bright as it had been when he first crawled his way out of the pod. Darkness was creeping in. This new situation led him to climb back into the safety of his pod, still clutching the apple that had fallen from the tree. His first day, had been incredible, so much to absorb, he felt fatigued. During the night, he heard a repetitive sound and a transparent colorless droplets ran down the pod. A word formed in his mind, the word was "rain". It was vital to maintain life.

When he got out of the pod, the next morning the rain had stopped and sunlight bathed the forest and it was as vibrant as the day before.

He dared to walk further. He knew he would have to start to eat the food that grew, from the land and trees. He decided to try to eat the apple. It was hard for him to bite, but the experiencing of tasting real food for the first time, left a strong impression on him. At first his stomach felt strange, it rejected the food. It took time for him to get used to it, but soon he was keen to find new things to eat, to discover new tastes. He soon discovered he was not the only living thing. He had stood for hours watching the running water of the river, which was not so far from where the pod was. He could see silvery shapes moving under the water. In time he would use them as a source of food. In the future he would teach himself how to make fire. It was essential to keep warm as darkness set in at night and the nights got colder. He was getting more used to living off the land and was moving more and more away from the pod. He built himself some kind of shelter, which managed to keep out the rain. He marveled at the birds and small insects that inhabited the earth. The land was rich, the forest so giving.

When he thought he had experienced all, he was presented with his first encounter with danger, a creature with a long tapering body, that let out a hissing sound. It was attached to a tree. It looked beautiful, but he instinctively sensed that creature could harm him. He had thrown a stone at it and ran, as quickly as he could. He realized he would have to be cautious, that the forest was not all good things. There was flaws even in paradise.

He began to swim, water had so many possibilities for him. This brought him great pleasure. He would then bask by the river as the sun beamed down. After a time he noticed changes in the weather and came to realization there were different seasons. Summer brought more fruit while winter was a time of hardship, of cold winds and animals seeking refuge.

He developed in so many ways. There was however an aspect of his development that

began to dog him, to gnaw away at his mind.
He was starting to feel alone, so terribly alone.
Little did he know that the human race had made
an abortive attempt to create a new quasi-world
on another planet, which had failed due to
malfunctions of the equipment. This left him, the
last representative of the human race, who went
by the name of Adam.